MARVEL
SIF

MARVEL

SIF

Even Dragons Have Their Endings

Book 2 of the Tales of Asgard Trilogy

Keith R.A. DeCandido

JOE BOOKS LTD

Published simultaneously in the United States and Canada
by Joe Books Ltd, 489 College Street, Toronto, Ontario, M6G 1A5

www.joebooks.com

Library and Archives Canada Cataloguing in Publication
information is available upon request

ISBN 978-1-772752-29-8 (print)
ISBN 978-1-988032-59-7 (ebook)

First Joe Books Edition: September 2016
3 5 7 9 10 8 6 4 2 1

For Meredith, whose heart is bigger than all the Nine Worlds combined.

"So comes snow after fire, and even dragons have their endings."

—J.R.R. Tolkien, *The Hobbit*

PRELUDE

The great world tree Yggdrasil sits at the center of the Nine Worlds, linking each world to the other eight.

The most populous of these worlds is Midgard, which its inhabitants refer to as Earth, but the most powerful denizens of the Nine Worlds reside in a different realm: Asgard. These immortals, ruled by the All-Father Odin, possess strength far beyond that of the mortal humans of Midgard.

Thousands of years ago, many Asgardians did cross the Bifrost—the rainbow bridge—to Midgard. The peoples of the region in which the Asgardians arrived saw the mighty immortals as gods, and so worshipped them. Today, some Asgardians still visit Midgard—particularly Thor the Thunderer, wielder of Mjolnir and master of the storms. In the modern age, he is viewed as one of many superheroes who protect humanity from chaos.

But as a youth, centuries before, Thor had been known as the protector of Asgard. The young god took his duties seriously, for he knew that such would continue to be his role as an adult when, as the son of Odin, he would take the throne of Asgard.

Odin knew of Thor's resolve, and so sent him to train

with his half brother, Tyr—the god of warfare. Also a son of Odin, Tyr was the greatest weapons master in all the Nine Worlds.

When young Thor left for his first lesson in swordplay with Tyr, however, he did not see that another followed— a girl in pigtails who stealthily tracked him to the Field of Sigurd.

Upon his arrival at the field, Thor was surprised to see not only the God of War, but also several other young men of Asgard. He recognized only one—a youth, blond like Thor, who went by the name of Fandral. All of the boys stood side by side, holding wooden swords.

"What deception is this?" the young god asked, confused. "I was told I would be taught by Tyr, yet I see a dozen others here."

Tyr laughed, tugging on his dark mustache. "Did you imagine, Thor, that you were the only boy in Asgard who wished to learn the craft of swordplay?"

"I suppose not." But Thor had hoped for private lessons from his half brother.

Tyr tossed Thor a wooden sword of his own. Thor caught it unerringly by the hilt and took his place in the line, right next to Fandral.

"Now then," Tyr said, "the first lesson is how to grip the weapon."

Over the next several weeks, Tyr taught the dozen boys

how to hold a sword properly—how to wield it in such a way that it could defend as well as attack, how to assume the proper ready position, and how to grip the sword when striking or parrying. He also paired up the students for practice drills and even had them spar a few times, giving points each time one struck the other with his wooden blade.

The sparring sessions were the only times that anyone was injured. Some of the students did not know their own strength—or their opponents had not taken Tyr's parrying lessons to heart. Of the two boys hurt, one was injured badly enough to no longer be able to fight; the other not badly at all, but his pride was sufficiently wounded that he refused to return.

And each day that Thor went to the field for his lesson, he was followed in secret by the girl in pigtails.

Finally, a month into Thor's training with the God of War, Tyr started the lesson with a lecture.

"Remember that the weapon you wield is only a tool. It is the heart of the one who wields it that will determine victory. All of you will grow up to be warriors of Asgard, and the women and children of the Realm Eternal will be relying upon you to protect them from our many enemies."

It was this statement that finally drove the girl to come out of hiding. She emerged from the other side of the large oak she had been taking refuge behind during the lessons and stood proudly before Tyr and his students, hands defiantly on her hips. "And what," she asked, "if the women prefer to defend themselves?"

Tyr smiled underneath his thick mustache. "At last you have revealed yourself."

Thor gaped. "Sif? Is that you?"

"Yes, Thor, it is I. And I find it strange that you and these other boys are deemed worthy of learning swordplay, but I am not."

Fandral laughed. "If so, girl, you're the only one who finds it so. Women are to be wooed and protected, after all."

Sif walked up to Fandral, and the latter was taken aback to realize that the girl was as tall as he was. "Boy, my name is 'Sif'—not 'girl.'"

"And I am Fandral, not 'boy.' You are Heimdall's sister, are you not?"

"I am."

Tyr interceded. "And she has been spying upon these lessons for quite some time. A true warrior, Sif, does not hide in the shadows. We are not dark elves or trolls who skulk about in darkness."

Turning to face Tyr, Sif said, "I might have asked to join the class, my lord, if I had believed for a moment that you would have consented."

"You know my mind that well, do you?" Tyr asked in an amused tone.

"When Thor first arrived, you asked if he was the only *boy* in Asgard who wished to master the sword." She indicated the dozen boys standing before her. "Your students are all boys."

"Boys who will one day become men who must fight for the Realm Eternal." Tyr shook his head. "I admire your spirit, Sif, but battle is important work—the work of men."

Sif stared up at Tyr's imposing presence. "Can only men do important work?"

"I did not—" Tyr started, but Sif would not let him interrupt her.

"Are the choosers of the slain not doing important work? The Valkyries were handpicked by Odin for their task— would you consider it unimportant? The Golden Apples of Immortality are kept by a woman, a task that is of sufficient import that we would lose our immortality were it not performed. Women bear the children that replace the warriors who fall in battle. Without them, Asgard would be empty. They who control our very destiny are women. I challenge you, Lord Tyr, to go to the Norns and tell them that the work they do is unimportant."

Tyr threw his head back and laughed. "Very well, little girl, you have made your point."

"Then I may join the class?"

"Of course not."

Thor stepped forward. "Why ever not, Lord Tyr?"

"Little Sif is a beautiful and wise girl—it would not do for her to injure herself."

Sif smiled. "I would worry more about my opponents."

"Nonetheless," Tyr said, "it is my class, and my rules."

"I have been observing your class since Thor joined it," Sif said, "and I have learned a great deal. I believe that I can defeat any of these boys in combat."

Fandral barked a laugh. "I sincerely doubt *that*, little girl. You may be able to make an argument, but that will do you little good in a battle of blades."

"More good than your boasting will, little boy," Sif said.

Tyr rubbed his chin. "Very well. Sif, you shall spar with Fandral. Best three touches out of five."

Fandral whirled on Tyr. "Why not first strike?"

Before Tyr could answer, Sif did so, quoting a past lesson: "Fortune may favor even the poorest warrior with a lucky shot."

"Indeed." Tyr spoke with respect, for the first time thinking that some of his words may well have been absorbed by the pigtailed girl.

Tyr grabbed one of the wooden swords and tossed it toward Sif, who caught it as unerringly as Thor had a month earlier.

Within a moment, the nine students and Tyr had formed a circle around Fandral and Sif, who faced each other. Each of them held their sword in a proper defensive position: blade pointed upward, ready to protect any part of the upper body.

Fandral moved around Sif, who moved only to stay facing Fandral at all times.

The boy grinned.

The girl did not.

Around them, most of the boys cheered Fandral on.

"Get her!"

"Hurry up and beat her, Fandral!"

"We'll never get back to classes at this rate! Thrash her!"

"Go, Fandral!"

"Beat the silly girl and get on with it!"

The one exception was Thor. Given his fellows' jeers, he decided to keep his peace. Though he bore Fandral no ill will, he was hoping for Sif's victory, for he did not share the belief held by his half brother and the other boys about a girl's place. Tyr, he felt, should welcome Sif into the class with open arms. After all, being a boy hadn't stopped two of the students from washing out of the class. Why not give a girl a chance? But then, Thor had been raised by Odin's wife, Frigga, and none would call *her* weak; if she presented a lesser aspect than Odin, it was only because everyone presented such an aspect when compared to the All-Father.

But Thor dared not say any of this aloud, knowing that it would only incur Tyr's wrath.

Eventually, Fandral's impatience cost him. After moving around Sif for the better part of a minute, he finally made the first move, an obvious swing that Sif parried easily.

They traded blows for several seconds—Fandral always attacking, Sif effortlessly parrying.

Realizing that Sif had been paying at least minimal attention to Tyr's lessons, Fandral redoubled his focus. He did several double and triple strikes, engaging in more complex maneuvers worthy of a proper opponent, which he belatedly realized that Sif most assuredly was.

Sif parried every strike.

Now Fandral grew frustrated and became more aggressive—so much so that he left his right side open with a two-handed left swing. Sif ducked that blow and simultaneously slid her blade sharply upward to touch the tip of her wooden sword to his ribs.

Tyr nodded. "One point for Sif."

Only then did Sif allow herself to smile.

As they returned to ready position, Fandral took a very deep breath through his nose and let it out through his mouth. It was a technique Tyr had taught them to keep control of themselves.

"Begin," Tyr said, and this time Fandral did not bother to circle, but attacked immediately.

Fandral's assault caught Sif off guard and she was unable to parry his second strike, his blade touching her hip.

"One point for each," Tyr said.

As they started their third round, Sif finally pressed an attack on Fandral. He had shown a tendency to raise his sword overhead far more often than was necessary, leaving himself vulnerable to low swings. So she waited for an opening, making sure to aim high in her initial attacks before switching to a low swing that caught Fandral completely unprepared.

"Two points for Sif, one point for Fandral."

To his credit, Fandral was more careful in the fourth round. Sif remained aggressive, but Fandral's defenses improved.

At one point, Sif slipped on some pebbles on the ground and barely managed to get her sword up in time as Fandral tried to take advantage. But as she tried to right herself, she fell again, and Fandral easily touched her leg with his sword.

"Two points each."

Thor stepped forward. "That was hardly fair, my lord! Sif slipped!"

"I wonder, half brother, if you did battle against a troll or a Frost Giant, and said to him, 'Wait! I slipped on a pebble and must right myself before we continue'—would it come to a good end for you?"

Sif said, "Thank you, Thor, but I accept the loss of the point. Life is seldom fair—if it were, I would not need to indulge in this charade to join the class."

Tyr nodded. "This shall be the final round. Whoever scores the point will win."

The opponents once again circled each other. Fandral

had taken Sif's measure, and found her to be far more skilled than he would have imagined. Sif had taken Fandral's measure, and found him to be intelligent and adaptable. It was no wonder that Tyr had put him up against her—Fandral was clearly the finest of Tyr's students.

For several seconds, they dueled tentatively. Fandral struck; Sif parried. They circled again. Sif struck; Fandral parried. And again they circled.

As time went on, the fight grew more aggressive. The final round lasted twice as long as any of the others had, with neither combatant able to gain an edge.

And then it was Fandral's turn to slip on rough ground, and Sif wasted no time in pressing her advantage, slipping her blade under his to strike on his shin.

Tyr, though, said nothing.

"That wasn't fair!" one of the boys cried.

"He slipped!"

"She can't win on a stupid technicality."

Thor whirled on the last boy. "I wonder, Egil, if you did battle against a Frost Giant or a dragon, and said to it, 'Wait! I slipped on a pebble and must right myself before we continue,'—would such a battle end well for you?"

"That isn't funny, Thor."

Before Thor could reply, Tyr said, "No, it is not." He folded his arms. "But, he is correct. Were I to deny Sif her victory, I must also take away Fandral's second point. Therefore I must grant victory—and ingress into the sword class—to Sif."

"Huzzah!" Thor cried, and Fandral also cheered from his prone position.

"Thank you, Thor." Sif reached out a hand to help Fandral up; the blond boy accepted. "I am surprised to hear your approbation, Fandral."

"Do not be, fair Sif, for even had I been victorious, I would have argued for your inclusion in Lord Tyr's lessons. Asgard would be poorly defended indeed if it did not utilize your skill with the blade."

Thor put a hand on Sif's shoulder, next to one of her dangling pigtails. "As Fandral says, so say I. Welcome, Sif, to our sword class."

"Thank you both." Then she bowed to Tyr. "And thank *you*, Lord Tyr."

"Do not thank me yet, young Sif, for you will either become one of the finest swordsmen—or rather, swordswomen—in the Nine Worlds, or you will return to your home ashamed and without honor."

"I have never gone home ashamed, my lord," Sif said. "Pray you, begin today's lesson."

"I would say," Thor said with a smile, "that the first lesson has already begun. We have all learned that a girl may best a boy with a blade."

"Perhaps," Tyr said. "But it is yet to be determined if a woman may do the same to a man."

CHAPTER ONE

Not far outside Asgard, beyond the Ida Plain and the Asgard Mountains, lay the Field of Sigurd. Once, Tyr, the older son of Odin, did teach the youth of Asgard how to fight, but, over the centuries, Tyr had become jealous of his half brother Thor, and did become an enemy of Asgard.

Thor himself had many a fond memory of his training. Once, he had adopted a civilian identity on Midgard in order to live amongst the humans and better protect them—for the people of Midgard were as much Thor's charge as were the people of Asgard—and the name he had chosen was Sigurd, after the very field where he had been taught the ways of combat.

On this day—millennia after Thor, Sif, and Fandral had trained there—young Hildegard, called Hilde, daughter of Volstagg the Voluminous, moved silently through the underbrush. Hiding behind one of the great oaks of the forest, she gazed upon the ground, trying to find the path of the stag she was tracking, which, based on the way the leaves were disturbed, had been this way recently.

At least, that was what she thought that disturbance meant.

She moved silently, touching the ground only with the balls of her feet, placing them carefully so they did not move the fallen leaves. The stag, unconcerned as it was with stealth, had not been as careful.

When she heard the sound of chewing, she realized she was close.

Not wishing to rush, Hilde moved behind a row of underbrush toward the sound, which grew louder as she approached. She took things slowly to ensure that she would perform her task properly.

Then she saw it.

No antlers, so it was a doe rather than a stag. The doe was stretching her long neck toward one of the trees, chewing on the leaves that jutted out from the ends of the lower branches.

Hilde noticed that most of the leaves in the doe's reach were gone. That meant Hilde now *did* have to rush, as the doe would be finished with her meal soon and would likely bound off, forcing Hilde to search again from scratch.

She walked up quietly behind the doe's rump, paused a moment to make sure the animal wouldn't move, and then touched the doe lightly. Surprised, the doe leapt an inch into the air and then bounded off.

From behind her, Hilde heard the sound of clapping, and a piercing alto voice rung out, echoing off the trees. "Well done, Hilde!"

Whirling around, Hilde saw the Lady Sif emerge from behind one of the trees. She had forgone her armor and was wearing simply a white tunic, black leggings, and boots, with her raven hair tied back. Her sword was sheathed at her side, and her hard face was softened by a bright smile.

"Were you following me the whole time?" Hilde asked.

"Of course. And you did very well, Hilde."

"Thank you, but—" Hilde shook her head, causing a few locks of red hair to fall into her eyes. "—how did you do it without me seeing you?"

Now Sif laughed. "Oh, Hilde, this past week I have taught *you* a great deal, but it is far from all that *I* know."

Lowering her head, Hilde said, "Of course."

"Still, you should be proud. None of the other students got as close to the target as you did."

"Really?" Hilde's face brightened, and visions of gloating over her siblings danced in her head.

"Come, let us rejoin the others."

Sif led Hilde to a large clearing—the very same clearing where Sif had won her way into Tyr's swordplay lessons as a child.

About a dozen children awaited them, all boys. Just as Sif had been the only girl in Tyr's charge, Hilde was the only girl in Sif's—though that was due to a dearth of volunteers, not by design. Indeed, Sif had hoped that more girls would ask to join the training, but only Hilde had done so.

The boys were seated around a campfire, and Sif was grateful to see that none of them had run away or done any damage to the camp. It helped that, each time she'd left to follow one of their peers who was testing their hunting skills, Sif had warned the group that if they misbehaved in any way, she would bring them before Odin himself, and they would be required to explain their behavior to the All-Father. That, it seemed, was enough to keep them in line.

They were loud, of course—asking a dozen boys to remain quiet was like asking a sun not to be hot—but at least they weren't shouting. Instead, they were telling each other stories, making fun of their peers, and speaking dismissively of adults—and discussing all of the other things boys talked about amongst themselves. Sif didn't care to know the specifics; she had had little patience with boys when she herself was a girl, and now she had even less.

Alaric, another of Volstagg's brood, saw Sif and Hilde approach, and got to his feet. "They're back! Hey, Lady Sif, how close did Hilde get? Not as close as me, I bet."

"No," Sif said, "she did not get as close as you."

That got a grin from Alaric. "Ha!"

Sif broke into a grin of her own, making Alaric's face fall. "She got closer."

"What?"

"In fact, Hilde is the only one of you to actually reach the target."

Shoulders now slumped, Alaric folded his arms angrily. "What do we need to know how to hunt for, anyway?"

"For food, obviously," said Bors, one of the grandchildren of Odin's aged Grand Vizier. He, and most of the other boys, had risen to his feet, excited about the news of Hilde's hunt.

Snorting, Alaric said, "If I want food, I'll ask Mother to cook something!"

Bors laughed right back. "I've seen your father—I doubt you need to ask your mother to cook."

Hilde strode forward. "Are you making fun of our parents?"

Stepping backward and holding up his hands, Bors quickly said, "Of course not, Hilde. I have nothing but respect for your parents, especially your father. Just please don't let him sit on me again!"

Sif held up her hands. "Enough! Everyone, be seated." The children returned to their places around the campfire, joined now by Sif and Hilde. Even seated, Sif towered over the children; while she did not have the height and breadth (and, in the case of Volstagg, the girth) of the male warriors she fought beside, she still was considerably larger than the youths of Asgard. "It is all well and good to know that you have hearth and home to rely upon for sustenance. But most of the battles of Asgard are not fought at home. On many occasions, I have found myself in need of provision while on a journey through the Nine Worlds to do battle on another plane.

"There was one occasion many centuries ago, when I was traveling to Niffleheim. I had brought jerky along to maintain my strength, but the journey proved longer than expected, and I had to ration my provisions. And then, when I came over a ridge, I was ambushed by a great beast."

One of the boys asked, "Was it Hilde's father?"

Bors shushed him.

"It was, in fact, a giant stag. I hadn't realized the creature was there, and it attacked as soon as it caught sight of me, attempting to gore me with its huge antlers."

"Did you beat it?" Bors asked.

Hilde rolled her eyes. "Of *course*, stupid, she's here telling the story, isn't she?"

"Oh, right."

"The *point*, little ones," Sif said in a menacing tone intended to forestall any more interruptions, "is that I was insufficiently aware of my surroundings. The stag out-weighed me by one and a half times—"

"It *was* the size of Father, then," Alaric muttered with a grin.

"—and I was unable to defeat it. It unhorsed me and I was barely able to hold it off with my sword while on foot. Eventually, I managed to put enough distance between me and the beast to get back to my horse, which was unharmed, and I rode away. I had traveled quite some distance before I realized that, when the stag had knocked my horse aside, it was not just I who fell from the steed's back, but also my pack. I had no supplies—and no food. What I learned that day was that while it is commendable to know how to defend yourself against foes, there are times when you must fend for yourself against the harsh realities of nature. And that is why I have been teaching you how to be aware of the creatures of the wilderness, and also how to approach them in secret and on foot. Had I known how to do such things on the road to Niffleheim, I might not have lost my provisions, nor would I have struggled to survive without them."

Sif looked around at her charges, hoping that she was getting through to them. Children were not Sif's favorite people in the Nine Worlds, as she found them mostly to be obnoxious and tiresome. Enough so that Sif had asked Odin why he had given her this particular assignment.

"Once," Odin had said in response to Sif's query, "my son Tyr took charge of teaching the youth of Asgard the way of the warrior—as you well know, Sif, having been his first female student."

Sif had nodded, trying not to let her pride show.

"But Tyr has long since abandoned Asgard, and in the aftermath of Hrungnir's attack, I believe it would be beneficial for one of my trusted warriors to take up Tyr's mantle."

"I would be honored," Sif had lied. "But why me?"

"You trained under Tyr. And yes, so did Thor and Fandral, but Thor is still recovering from injuries suffered at Hrungnir's hands, and I do not believe that Fandral has the patience and discipline required to be a teacher of children."

"While I would agree with the All-Father regarding Fandral, would those sentiments not apply equally as well to me?" Sif had asked in a tone that made it clear that the answer to her question was yes.

Odin, however, had not taken the bait. "I believe, Sif, that you underestimate yourself. Besides, I recall you were not shy in your criticisms of Tyr's methods. Here is your chance to, as the mortals of Midgard say, put your money where your mouth is."

Over the millennia, Sif had seen Odin angry, haughty, strong, righteous, and frightening. Which was why his rare forays into mischievousness always gave her pause, as it had on this occasion.

He was right, however, as she *had* had issues with Tyr's methods. That was why she had insisted on hunting being part of the children's training. There was far more to being a warrior than swordplay, something she learned only after Tyr's tutelage had ended—and despite it, not because of it. She would not allow the younger ones of Asgard to have to learn the hard way, as she had.

Looking at her pupils around the campfire, she continued with her lesson. "As you all know, the giant Hrungnir recently attacked Asgard."

"Why did he attack Asgard, anyhow?" Bors asked.

Sif sighed. They had just finished a long day of training, and the sun would be setting soon. It was, perhaps, the appropriate time to tell a story before they bedded down for the night; they would hike back to Asgard on the morrow.

"One day," she said, "a group of trolls attacked Asgard. Their way was paved by Loki, the Trickster, when he gave them a path that even my all-seeing brother, Heimdall, could not espy. And so they reached the very heart of the city before a defense could be mustered."

"That was you and Father, right?" Hilde asked. "The defense?"

"'Twas I, yes, along with Volstagg, as well as Thor and Balder, and your father's boon companions, the Warriors Three—Fandral and Hogun. The battle was—" Sif hesitated. "—*complicated* by more treachery from Loki. He hid Mjolnir from Thor, and left a false hammer in its place. But even denied Thor's greatest weapon, together we did rout the trolls and expose Loki's perfidy. The Trickster was brought before Odin and punished by being confined to his keep for a month—where still he sits."

"I don't understand," said Lars, another of the children. Sif suspected that the boy started many a sentence with those three words. "What does the trolls' attack have to do with Hrungnir?"

Sif recalled that Lars had never gotten within a league of his prey during his own hunting test, and she told him now what she had told him then: "Patience, Lars."

Lars sulked. "Okay."

"After having to punish his own son, Odin set out in disguise on his mighty steed, Sleipnir. While so doing, he encountered Hrungnir, who had a great steed of his own, Goldfaxi. From astride Goldfaxi, Hrungnir led his band of Frost Giants to menace the countryside in Jotunheim and Nornheim. Hrungnir did challenge Odin to a race of their steeds, though Hrungnir knew not that he was challenging the All-Father."

"Sleipnir won, right?" Hilde said urgently.

Sif smiled. "Of course. Odin's horse is the fastest in all the Nine Worlds, and there was no doubt that he would win the race against Goldfaxi. But at no point did Odin reveal himself, and Hrungnir did abide by the terms of their contest and let him go on his way. But somehow, the giant discovered that he had lost to the ruler of Asgard, and thought that Odin had played him for a fool. And so he brought his forces to bear on Asgard itself. Again, Thor, the Warriors Three, Balder the Brave, and I rallied to Asgard's defense, confronting the Frost Giants on the Ida Plain."

Alaric said, "That's when we went to the mountains!"

"Yes," said Sif with a nod to Volstagg's son. "Odin felt that the children of Asgard needed to be safeguarded, for Hrungnir had brought a larger contingent of combatants than the trolls had brought. And so he sent you all with his wife, Frigga, and your mother, Gudrun, into the mountains and to safety in the Vale of Crystal. But, as you recall, when Hrungnir made his cowardly retreat from the Ida Plain, he took the same route to Jotunheim that you children had taken through the mountains. Frigga confronted Hrungnir and kept you safe, but the giant did defeat her and take her hostage."

Hilde said, "I wish we could have helped her. Maybe then she wouldn't have been captured!"

"Indeed, young Hilde, and that is why Odin asked me to work with all of you. The children of Asgard may someday be called upon to aid in its defense. Plus, many of you will grow up to become warriors of Asgard. You must be prepared."

"Hey," Bors said, "what happened to Frigga? I mean, I know she got home safe, but how?"

"I heard the Warriors Three raided Jotunheim!"

"I heard Thor wiped out all the Frost Giants with his hammer!"

"I heard Odin smote them all!"

"In fact," Sif said loudly to cut off more speculation from the children, "the giants had a ransom for the Lady Frigga.

Hrungnir would free her if Thor faced him in one-on-one combat. However, the giant did not reveal that he wore enchanted stone armor until Thor arrived. But still, Thor was victorious, though he remains abed, recovering from the grievous wounds inflicted upon him by the Frost Giant."

"Wow," Bors said.

The sun was starting to set; Sif looked at the children. "And now night begins to fall, so it is time to see who has learned their lessons best, for we must have our evening repast."

"What's it gonna be?" Alaric asked, licking his lips.

"That depends entirely upon all of you. Now that you have learned huntcraft, you must go out and obtain our dinner using your new skills."

The faces of all the children fell—except, Sif noted, for Hilde's, which instead smiled with anticipation.

Sif had a feeling that she knew who would be providing tonight's meal. And of course, if they all failed, Sif herself would hunt. But what better way to test the children than to give them a task they were motivated by hunger to complete?

CHAPTER TWO

The first time Sif went to visit Thor after he was injured by Hrungnir, the thunder god was in relatively good spirits. He had rescued his mother, and Hrungnir had been utterly defeated. Not only had he been routed in the battle with Thor, but he had also lost the leadership of the Frost Giants.

With each subsequent visit, however, Thor's demeanor grew surlier.

"Good morrow, Thor!" Sif said upon entering his bedchamber, where he had lain for the better part of a fortnight.

"There is little I find to be good about it," Thor muttered.

Concerned, Sif asked, "Are your wounds not healing?"

"The healers do make their noises about progress, and I can indeed feel the slow process of bones mending."

"Then what is the issue?"

"It is taking so *long*!"

Sif could not help but laugh.

Bemused, Thor asked, "Does the thunder god's agony amuse the Lady Sif?"

"It does, actually." She sat at his bedside and put her hand on Thor's. "You have fought a great battle, Thor—one that will be spoken of at feasts and celebrations for millennia to come. But all battles have a price, and you are paying it now. You were once a mortal physician—you should be aware of precisely how long it will take for such injuries as you sustained to right themselves."

At that, Thor did allow himself a smile. "It is a saying on Midgard that doctors are the worst patients. It would seem that I am proving that maxim, even if I am no longer truly a human healer."

Shaking her head, Sif said, "If Tyr could see you now . . ."

Thor barked a laugh. "Ah, my half brother would not have a kind word for me under any circumstances."

Remembering an incident not long ago when Tyr did battle with Thor in an attempt to win her affections, Sif shuddered. Tyr's unwillingness to consider Sif's wishes had remained a theme throughout their interactions, from his initial refusal to allow her into his sword-fighting class to his mistaken belief that defeating Thor would cause her to fall into Tyr's arms.

"But enough of my own unseemly complaints." Thor sat up straighter in the bed. "You have obviously returned from training the children. How fared them?"

"Some better than others." Sif told Thor of their adventures—including the success of Hilde and some of the others, and the failures of the remainder.

"Be watchful, Sif, or Hildegard shall eclipse you as the finest shield-maiden in Asgard."

Sif chuckled. "If it were to be so, I would be honored—for as children go, Hilde is almost tolerable."

Before the conversation could continue, a knock came at the front door to Thor's home.

"Are you expecting anyone?" Sif asked.

"None who would feel the need to knock. Only the healers or my boon companions come, and they may enter freely."

Sif rose from the bed. "I will determine who this strange visitor might be, then."

She approached the front door and opened it to a small, young man with a very thin beard, who was drenched in sweat and who breathlessly asked, "Is Thor at home? I was told that he'd be here!"

"Be calm, my friend. Thor is indeed at home, but in poor condition to receive visitors whom he does not know."

"Forgive me, lady, but I *must* see the thunder god! I am Frode from the village of Flodbjerge. Thor is the only hope to save us!"

Sif smiled wryly. "Then Flodbjerge may well be doomed, for Thor is badly injured. He is not to leave his bed for another fortnight, at least."

Frode's face fell. "Oh, no! All is lost! Please, may I at least see him, so I may tell my doomed fellow villagers that I did at least witness that Thor was unable to come to us in our hour of need?"

"Of course." Sif led the nervous young man in. As they moved through Thor's home to the bedroom, she added, "You are aware, are you not, that there are other warriors in Asgard who might serve to defend your village?"

"I cannot speak to that, milady, only that I was charged with contacting Thor as soon as possible!"

"And so you have," said Thor, for that last phrase was said as Frode entered the thunder god's bedchamber. "What message is it that you bring to Thor Odinson?"

Bowing before the foot of Thor's bed, Frode said, "I am Frode of the village of Flodbjerge. For a fortnight now, we have been attacked regularly by a dragon! We have attempted to defend ourselves, but the dragon is far too mighty for those such as us to do battle with, and several of our towns-folk have lost their lives. We require the God of Thunder's strong right arm and mighty hammer, Mjolnir!"

Thor sighed. "Would that I could help you—but as you can see, I am in no condition to answer my own door, much less fly to your aid. But you may take heart, noble Frode, for there is another in this very room whose strong right arm is the equal of mine own."

Frode leapt to his feet and gaped at Sif. "Your maid?"

Sif glowered at Thor for a moment, and then turned her attention to Frode. "I am the Lady Sif, young Frode. I serve at the pleasure of no one, save for Odin himself."

Frode once again fell to his knees, but this time was fully prostrate. "My lady! Please accept the deepest apologies of your humble servant, for I did not know 'twas you."

Shaking her head, Sif said, "Rise, Frode, for the fault is not your own. One would not expect a warrior of Asgard to be answering doors—your mistake is understandable and easily forgiven."

Getting slowly and cautiously to his feet, Frode said, "Thank you, my lady. You are too kind."

"As for your problem, I have just spent a week performing a task that has been, shall we say, far from my first choice in activity. I believe that doing battle with a dragon will be far more palatable. Besides, it has been centuries since last I fought such a creature."

Thor smiled, recalling Sif's fight against a dragon on Midgard a millennium ago. "You may rest assured, Frode, that there are few in the Nine Worlds better suited to save your town from this foul beast. I'm sure the Lindworm of Denmark would attest to that, were it able to speak from Hel."

"We are honored. The Lady Sif is renowned in song and story as one of Asgard's finest warriors. I would be privileged to bring you back with me, milady."

Sif nodded to Frode, and then went to Thor's bedside. "Be well, Thor."

"I shall. Your company shall again be missed, but I have no doubt that Volstagg will be present ere long to bring me food and then eat it all himself while he regales me with exaggerated tales of his exploits."

"Of course he will. You are a captive audience—Volstagg's favorite kind." Sif smiled and kissed Thor on the forehead.

"I expect that you will return known once again as Sif Dragonslayer," Thor said.

"Perhaps." She turned to the man from Flodbjerge. "Come, Frode, let us be away!"

CHAPTER THREE

Flodbjerge, not too far from Asgard, was located at the base of the Valhalla Mountains. To get there, Sif and Frode had to traverse along the Gopul River on foot. Sif had taken the time to change into her red armor and white headpiece, which served to keep her dark hair out of her face. She had considered and rejected the notion of taking along the cloak—Flodbjerge was warm this time of year, and she suspected that the cloak would merely get in the way.

"Many of our horses have been wounded or killed by the dragon," Frode had explained with regard to his coming to Asgard without a mount. "The few able-bodied ones that remain were deemed too valuable to risk on a journey to Asgard."

As Sif clambered over a large rock that blocked their path, she said, "I understand why. The passage to your village is not suitable for any but the heartiest of steeds."

Even as they continued on foot along the Gopul, Sif noticed that they were not alone. Someone had followed them from Asgard, but Sif decided that the trail was difficult enough that eventually their pursuer would have no choice but to reveal herself. She kept her counsel for the time being, not wishing to worry Frode. While the young man was abject in his insistence that Sif was a perfectly adequate substitute for Thor, Sif also knew that the rest of the villagers might not think the same.

She had dealt with such idiotic disappointment more times than she was able to count. "But you're just a *woman!*" "You're not Thor." "But there are *three* of the Warriors Three!" "You seem rather, well, *small* for a warrior." "They call you a shield-maiden—shouldn't you be carrying a shield instead of that heavy sword?" And so on.

When the western bank of the Gopul was no longer passable, Sif and Frode looked to cross to the eastern bank, which opened up to a wide plain that Frode said would lead directly to Flodbjerge. Looking up, Sif could see the Valhalla Mountains, at the base of which was located the village.

They chose a crossing where the river was at its narrowest, and where several rocks that were larger than the river was deep allowed easy passage across.

"It shouldn't be long now," Frode said as he leapt onto one of the rocks. "Be wary, milady, as the first rock is slippery."

"Thank you." Sif followed him, making sure to keep herself sure footed as her boot landed on the wet stone.

A minute later, when she and Frode were most of the way across the river, Sif heard a small scream and a splash.

Turning, Sif looked down with amusement at the tiny form of Volstagg's daughter Hilde, flailing her arms and legs in the river, her red hair plastered damply to her head. The girl had slipped on the first rock.

Leaping back a few rocks, Sif smiled down at Hilde. "And you were doing so well up to that point."

"You knew I was following you?" Hilde asked, treading water.

"As I said, Hilde, I have not come close to teaching you all that *I* know." Sif reached out her hand.

Hilde grabbed Sif's hand and allowed herself to be pulled out of the water. Sif guided her to the eastern bank, where Frode was waiting.

"Who is this?" Frode asked, confused.

"Hildegard, daughter of Volstagg the Voluminous. Hilde, this is Frode of Flodbjerge."

To her credit, Hilde attempted to curtsy, though it was difficult, as her bulky brown tunic and black leggings were quite waterlogged.

Introductions finished, Sif looked down at Hilde. "Why have you followed us?"

"Um . . ." Hilde looked away. "I've never seen a dragon before."

"I should send you back to Asgard."

"Please don't!" Hilde grabbed Sif's armor and looked up at her with a pleading expression. "I want to see the dragon! And I want to help! You spent all that time teaching us—I want to put what I've learned to good use!"

Sif shook her head. "You realize that if anything happens to you, your father will likely sit on me until I expire."

"He won't! I promise! Besides, I can take care of myself!"

Frode spoke up. "Milady, we must hurry."

Shaking her head, Sif pulled Hilde's wet hands off her armor. "Oh, very well. It's probably more dangerous for you to find your way back across the Gopul without me keeping an eye on you."

Hilde grinned. "I thought I was keeping an eye on *you*."

"Ha!" Sif chuckled. "However, you're not going anywhere near the dragon. Come, let us tarry no longer."

"We will be there within the hour," Frode said. "I fear that Oter will attack again soon."

"Oter is the dragon?" Sif asked. Frode had been parsimonious with details up to this point, so focused was he on his mission to return to his village with a warrior. Sif knew she would get the details soon enough, and regardless, it wasn't as if she would refuse to help the town.

"Yes, milady. He named himself the first time he attacked. 'I am Oter,' he cried, and then exhaled his unholy, flaming breath upon us. However, those three words are the only ones he has spoken aloud."

"How often does he attack?" Sif asked.

"There has been no pattern to it, but what is most passing strange is that he turns his attention to a different portion of the village on each occasion." Frode shook his head sadly. "Our village will be naught but a cinder soon, unless you stop him, milady."

Sif had no response to that, and so instead asked the next obvious question. "Where does the dragon come from?"

"The mountains, milady—but a more specific location, I could not say. Fast is Oter, and wily. He comes from a different spot within the Valhalla Mountains on each occasion, and we cannot see his destination when he departs because of all the smoke caused by his foul breath."

Hilde spoke, having spent much of her time since they had crossed the river trying and failing to wring the water from her soaked clothes. "We should try to track the dragon. Perhaps we can beard Oter in his lair!"

Regarding Hilde dubiously, Sif said, "'We' shall do no such thing, young Hilde."

"But you said my tracking skills were excellent!"

"Of a deer, which does walk through the forest upon hooves that leave distinct marks upon the ground. How, pray, shall you track a dragon through the air?"

Hilde looked down, abashed. "I hadn't thought of that."

"In any case, child, it is I who shall do any bearding."

Frode pointed and said, "There it is!"

Turning, Sif followed his finger and spied the village. Several small structures lined the river, with larger ones a bit farther inland. Sif also saw many boats in the river, all close to a natural port at the water's widest point.

As they drew closer, Sif observed that many of the structures were burnt and pitted; there were also many piles of wood, ash, and stone that had likely once been buildings.

"We have been fortunate thus far," Frode said, "in only one way—the dragon has yet to turn his attention on our fishing boats."

Hilde smiled. "My father has often spoken very highly of the fish from Flodbjerge."

For the first time since Sif met him, she saw a smile on Frode's visage. "High praise indeed from Asgard's finest epicure."

Sif noticed a boathouse that seemed abandoned—but also not burnt. "What of this structure?"

"The Gopul overflowed last spring and caused water damage to the boathouse. It was always too small for the purpose in any case, and so we built a new one farther north. This boathouse is no longer used."

Two women and one man ran toward them as they passed the abandoned boathouse. "Is he coming?" the man asked breathlessly.

"The God of Thunder is unavailable," Frode said.

One of the women said, "You were told to bring Thor."

Sif stepped forward. "Thor was badly injured in battle with the Frost Giants. I am the Lady Sif, and I promise I shall defend your village from this scourge."

Both women looked up at Sif with awe. "We are honored, milady."

"Thank you for agreeing to defend our village."

The man, though, frowned at her. "I thought you'd be taller."

"When did Oter last attack?" Sif asked, pointedly ignoring the man.

Before anyone could answer her question, a voice cried out from the direction of the port. "The dragon is back!"

Amid the screams, wails, and curses that followed, Sif turned back toward the river and saw in the distance a green-scaled form winging its way toward the village. In the small amount of time it took her to register the dragon's presence, it was almost on top of the port.

Quickly, Sif brandished her sword and sprinted toward the river. She ran as fast as she could, but the dragon had already reached the port and was breathing fire upon the fishing boats, the occupants leaping into the water in order to save themselves from the flames.

The dragon flew up into the air and circled around to take another pass at the port.

Sif kept running, but slowed her pace so she would reach the water's edge at just the right moment, and, as Oter made a low pass near the river, again breathing fire at the fishing boats, leapt onto the creature's left wing.

The wing was about twice as long as Sif's height, and her extra weight caused Oter to list to the left, nearly plummeting into the river. Sif plunged her sword into the creature's wing and Oter screamed, fire blasting from his maw.

The dragon flailed. Sif yanked out her sword and struggled to gain purchase on the wing. Green blood oozed from the wound and dripped down the wing, making it slick to the touch. Sif felt herself slipping.

"You will trouble this village no longer, dragon!" she cried as she attempted to clamber along the wing toward Oter's body.

The dragon craned its head toward Sif, staring at her with huge, yellow eyes underneath two large horns protruding from his forehead. He replied in a deep, resonant voice that sounded as though it came from Hela's domain. "If I cease, it shan't be thanks to your pitiful doing!"

With that, Oter dove straight for the river, breaking through the water's surface.

Water smashed into Sif's body and she struggled to both breathe and hold on to both the dragon and her sword.

She maintained her grip on her sword, but when the dragon broke through the river's surface to once again take to the sky, Sif was left behind in the water, along with the many fishermen who had abandoned their boats.

She swam to the surface, and upon breaking through,

found that fewer of the boats were on fire than had been before Oter dove underwater. No doubt the creature's displacement of the river had soaked many of them, thus negating the dragon's work.

Of the creature himself, she saw no sign. His speed was as great as Frode had indicated, and the dragon was already long out of sight.

"Next time, Oter," Sif muttered under her breath.

As Sif started to swim toward the port, she heard a familiar voice cry out, "Don't just *stand* there, get those rafts moving!"

It was Hilde, directing the villagers, who Sif saw were standing stunned at the devastation wrought by Oter.

Frode was the first to act on Hilde's words, saying, "She's right—we must retrieve those people before they drown!"

"Help!" a voice cried from behind Sif. She whirled around to see two people, a man and a woman, struggling to stay afloat.

Quickly, Sif swam toward them and grabbed both of them, one in each arm. "Hold on," she said, and used her powerful legs to kick toward the shore. It was much slower going without the use of her arms, but she managed to get them all safely to the port.

Frode and two other men were waiting for her, and they pulled the two people out of the water. Once they were safely on dry land, Sif hauled herself up—her armor now even more soaked than Hilde's clothes had been after she had fallen into the river earlier.

Over the next hour, Sif helped retrieve those who remained in the water. At one point, she noticed Hilde helping people off a boat that had been docked during the dragon's raid. Sif walked over to Volstagg's daughter, who was giving a blanket to a soaking-wet child, and asked, "Was this boat attacked, as well?"

Hilde nodded. "It's the only one that was in dock that was hit. Bad luck."

As night fell over Flodbjerge, a boy ran up to Sif. "Excuse me, milady?"

"Yes?" Sif knelt down so she was eye to eye with him.

"I bear a message from the village council. They're ready to see you, as requested."

"Excellent." Sif stood. "Where?"

The boy pointed.

Sif followed the boy's finger to the town's meeting hall. Or rather, what was left of it. The walls were made of stone, but there was still considerable fire damage, and the roof had been destroyed.

"Can I come with you?" Hilde asked as they approached the hall.

Shaking her head, Sif said, "No, Hilde, I wish you to aid the healers. Many were injured."

Hilde rolled her eyes. "Anyone can do that."

"Perhaps." Sif stopped and looked down at Hilde, putting a hand on her shoulder. "But look at these people, Hilde. Their homes have been destroyed, and they've spent the past several weeks cleaning up after repeated vicious attacks. They're exhausted. I believe that the sight of a strong, young woman of Asgard who does *not* walk around as if she's already been defeated will do wonders to help the injured get well."

"All right," Hilde said. "I want to help."

"This task will help immensely."

Nodding, Hilde ran off.

Sif entered the hall. Without a roof, the inside was just as cool as the outside now that the sun had set. Stools had been brought over from the tavern—also a burnt, pitted wreck—as the hall's furniture had been destroyed by the dragon.

The council included Frode, two other men—Bjorn and Olaf—and one woman, Helena. Olaf and Helena were two of the trio who had greeted Sif on her arrival—Olaf was the one who'd expected her to be taller. The third person she'd met was Bjorn's wife, who was the town healer, and was well occupied elsewhere in the wake of Oter's carnage.

Helena spoke first. "To begin, Lady Sif, may I express the gratitude of all of Flodbjerge for your assistance today. Several of our people would have died had you not driven off the dragon so soon, and then aided in the rescue efforts."

"Of course," Sif said with a bow of her head. "Although I am not entirely convinced that I was the cause of the dragon's departure. But, of course, I am pleased to aid you in whatever way possible."

"Again, thank you."

"To that end," Sif continued, "I would like to know the full story of how the dragon came to beset you. Frode began to tell me, but the dragon's attack curtailed his account."

"Of course," Helena said, and turned to Bjorn.

Bjorn leaned forward on the stool. "We have always been a quiet, peaceful village, and have relied these many centuries on the protection of Asgard and Lord Odin. We sustain ourselves through trade, as the fish in our waters are considered delicacies by most of the Nine Worlds. While oftentimes our citizens have been conscripted to do battle against Asgard's foes—for example, many citizens of Flodbjerge fought against Surtur's minions—for the most part, we have lived our lives in peace. That changed a fortnight ago, when Oter first attacked."

Frode shuddered. "It was horrible."

Nodding, Bjorn continued. "That first time was a bright, sunny day, much like any other. Midday here is our most active time—the boats have come in from the river, and the daily catches are being sorted and stored. It was, in fact, *right* at midday when the dragon first appeared."

Bjorn closed his eyes and exhaled slowly. This was clearly

difficult for him to remember, and Sif felt a pang of regret for asking, but she needed the information. Tyr may have taught her how to wield a sword, but it was through her own millennia of experience in battle that she had learned the best weapon in warfare was intelligence. It wasn't enough to know that a dragon attacked the village. She needed details of how, which might lead to why. And why might lead to another how—to wit, how to stop Oter.

Finally, Bjorn went on. "He seemed to come from nowhere. One moment, we were sorting the fish, the next he was upon us, his girth blocking out the sun as he descended."

Helena shuddered. "He destroyed an entire section of the village."

Leaning forward, Sif asked, "Which section?"

"Does it matter?" Helena was confused at the query.

"It might."

Olaf said, "The northeast corner of Flodbjerge. Four houses near each other. It was only those four, and then he departed."

"And after that?" Sif asked.

Olaf looked helplessly at Sif. "After that, what?"

"I must know where Oter attacked each time."

The council exchanged glances with each other.

Urgently, Sif asked, "Can you show me on a map?"

"Of course." Helena rose from her stool and walked to a

table that held several scrolls, a few codex books, and a large map.

Sif joined her.

Helena pointed at the map's northeastern section. "That is where the first attack occurred." She pointed at a place a bit farther west, but still on the town's northern edge. "Then here." Then the northwestern corner. "Then here."

The pattern Helena described indicated that the dragon was moving methodically through the village—almost in a grid.

Almost, because it had skipped two sections. One was near the center of town, which should have come after the attack that damaged the meeting hall and the tavern. The other, on the town's northern outskirts, should have been the third place raided. "He didn't attack either of these two spots. What are they?"

Pointing to the northernmost section, Helena said, "There are four houses there that were destroyed in an avalanche last winter—the same has happened five times in the last decade and the families who lived there chose to rebuild their homes elsewhere. We have all agreed to leave that area free from construction.

Frode indicated the section nearer to where they now sat. "This is our storehouse. It is kept cold by spells we acquired from Niffleheim, and our winter stores are kept there so that we may eat even when the Gopul River freezes over."

"So there are no people in either place?"

Olaf shook his head. "No one uses the storehouse in these warm months, no. Why?"

Sif nodded. "It makes sense. I believe that Oter is not attempting to destroy your village."

"That's absurd!" Bjorn said. "How else do you explain what has happened?"

"If he wished to destroy Flodbjerge, he could have done so the first day he blotted out the sun and ravaged the northeast corner of your village. But he did not. Instead, he has been moving methodically, predictably. Indeed, I can say most assuredly that he will next set his sights upon this collection of structures along the riverbank." She placed a finger on the grid, showing where the next attack would occur.

"The repair shop." Frode shook his head. "That is the facility where our seacraft are taken for repair when they are damaged. Much of the equipment stored there is unique and would be difficult to replace."

"Then I suggest you remove those items, and quickly," Sif said sternly.

"But wait," Bjorn said, "he *hasn't* been moving predictably. Like you said, he skipped the three homes and the storehouse."

"Yes. Because I believe that he is not out to destroy—he is searching for someone. Oter is in the mountains, and therefore has an excellent vantage point from which to observe your comings and goings. But he must be searching for a specific person, and so he is checking each of the populated areas. He is skipping those parts of Flodbjerge that are uninhabited because they do not serve his purpose."

"But for whom does the dragon search?" Olaf asked.

Sif shook her head, sadly. "I do not know. But if we are to learn that person's identity, we would be well to do so with dispatch."

CHAPTER FOUR

When she had woken up that morning, Hilde had had no intention of following Sif in an attempt to assist her. In fact, after spending a week in training with her, she'd had no intention of seeing Sif again for a very long while.

But then Alaric had been an idiot.

Years ago, when she was very small, Hilde had seen her father's collection of hunting knives for the first time. One in particular caught her eye because of the intricately carved dragon design on the hilt. Volstagg had told her that it was his second-best hunting knife, the one he had used when he, Fandral, and Hogun had gone after the Fenris Wolf. His best hunting knife was the one Gudrun had given him as a wedding gift—and Volstagg would never part with it—but he did that day promise to gift Hilde the dragon-hilt knife when she was old enough to use it properly.

Upon returning home from her week with Sif, Hilde had been hoping that now would be the time for that gift. And then she had checked her father's collection, and had seen that the dragon-hilt knife was gone.

Hilde had been devastated, so she had gone to her mother.

"Oh," Gudrun had said, "your father is hoping it can be

repaired, I think. Something about Alaric using it on a hard-wood tree."

"What!?"

Livid, Hilde had sought out her brother. "Did you use my hunting knife?"

Alaric had stared at her, confused. "You have a hunting knife?"

"The one with the dragon carved on the handle! Father promised it to me!"

"Why would he do *that*? Anyhow, I needed it to cut down that hardwood tree on the lawn."

Hilde had been unsure which appalled her more, that he was dumb enough to think a hunting knife was the right tool for cutting down a tree, or that he had used *her* hunting knife.

So she jumped him.

They'd scuffled for a few minutes before Mother broke up the fight. "What in the name of all the Nine Worlds are you two *doing*?"

Alaric—doubled over and clutching his stomach, as Hilde had gotten in a good punch to his solar plexus—had said, "She just hit me for no reason!"

"Is that true, Hilde?" Gudrun had asked her.

"No, it's not." Then Hilde had looked away. "I had a very *good* reason. He ruined my hunting knife!"

"How is it *yours*?" Alaric had asked yet again.

"Father promised it to me!"

"Well, don't worry—the smith'll probably fix it."

"*Probably?*" Hilde had almost jumped him again, but a look from her mother stopped her.

Gudrun had stared down angrily at both of them. "Go to your rooms, both of you. And don't come out until supper."

Hilde had no idea whether Alaric had acceded to Mother's request to stay in his room, but Hilde hadn't lasted more than five minutes before climbing out the window to seek out the Lady Sif.

Mother didn't understand. That was *Hilde's* knife! Father had *promised* it to her!

She quickly found out that Sif had gone to visit Thor, and Hilde had arrived just as Frode was explaining about the dragon.

Since returning home would have incurred Mother's wrath, she decided to go with Sif. But Sif wouldn't have given Hilde permission to come along if Hilde had asked. She instead followed a dictum that she'd learned from two of her adopted brothers, Kevin and Mick, who, although born and raised on Midgard, had been taken in by Volstagg and Gudrun upon being orphaned: "It's easier to obtain forgiveness than permission."

Besides, Sif would be so much more impressed if Hilde used her hunting skills to track Sif and her companion!

Hilde hadn't expected Sif to know she was there all along,

but she should have guessed Sif would know. Either way, she was grateful that the lady had let her stay.

Now, Hilde was helping gather the debris from one of the destroyed boats that had been brought to shore. She couldn't carry much—Hilde was small, and most of the others were bigger and stronger than she was—but she was fast and agile, so she made up in speed what she lacked in strength.

When she brought the last pile of debris to the shed, where it would be sorted through to see what was still useful and what would only be good as kindling, a man approached her.

"Excuse me—you're the girl who came with the Lady Sif, yes?"

Hilde looked up to see a tall, gaunt man wearing only black—tunic, pants, boots, belt—all entirely black. Hilde found it to be rather depressing. Most of the occupants of Flodbjerge wore muted earth-and-jewel tones—probably because these didn't look as bad when they got wet. The man had a very thin beard and short dark hair.

"Yes, I'm Hildegard." She used her full name, figuring it would make her sound more like a woman of Asgard than a child of it, never mind how small she was.

"Good. I need to speak with the Lady Sif immediately. Do you know where I can find her?"

At first, Hilde opened her mouth to tell the man where to find Sif, but then she stopped. "Why do you need to know?"

"I *must* see her."

She stared at the man's hands and clothes. They were all clean and pristine, except for his boots, but even they had only mild scuffing on them. "Have you been helping with the cleanup?"

The man hesitated. "I'm sorry?"

"This town was just attacked by a *dragon*. Maybe you saw it?"

"Of course I did! Look, Hildegard—"

"Your clothes and hands are clean. You haven't been helping, have you?"

Again, the man hesitated. "If someone had asked—"

"You needed to be *asked*? Nobody asked *me* to help—I don't even live here—but I volunteered, because I thought it was *important*."

"Then you're a very good girl. Your parents must be proud."

Hilde didn't respond to that, as her parents were probably wondering where she was and worried sick about her at this point. But in general, the man was right—she knew that both Volstagg and Gudrun were proud of her. And so was Sif—she had all but said so after Hilde had touched the doe's rump.

Aloud, though, Hilde said only, "Why should I take you to see Sif?"

The man took a breath. "My name is Regin. I only recently moved to this village."

"Okay. Is that why you think you're exempt from helping out? I know if *I* had just moved somewhere, I'd want everyone to like me and want me to stay because I pitched in whenever something went badly."

Regin let out a long breath. "Perhaps. But I prefer to keep a low profile. You see, I came to this village because it's quiet and out of the way, and I like to keep to myself."

"They've been under attack by a dragon for *weeks*. I really think—"

"Look, *little* girl," Regin said in a tone of great impatience, "are you going to take me to Sif or not?"

"I'm still waiting for you to answer my question."

Regin frowned. "What question?"

"Why should I take you to see her?"

A third hesitation, then he finally said, "I have information she will need to combat the dragon."

Hilde blinked. "What?"

"I said—"

"I heard what you said. If you know about the dragon, why haven't you told anyone else?"

"I told you, I like to keep to myself. I very rarely leave the rooms I rent. And at first, I didn't see the dragon. I just heard—and sometimes felt—the attacks, and later listened to the stories people told about them. But until today, I never actually *saw* it." Regin closed his eyes for a moment, then reopened them. "My bedchamber window looks out on the docks, and today I saw the dragon quite clearly. And I recognized it as Oter."

"We *know* his name is Oter."

That surprised Regin. "I'm sorry?"

"According to the town council, he called himself Oter the first time he attacked."

"Hm." Regin rubbed his bearded chin. "Well, in any case, I need to inform Sif of what I know. Trust me, she will want to hear this."

"Fine." Hilde started toward the town hall. Maybe Sif and the council were done with their meeting, in any case.

Sure enough, as Hilde and Regin approached the town hall, Sif and another woman were exiting the building. Hilde recalled that this was Helena, the head of the town council.

"Sif!" Hilde cried out. "This man wants to talk to you!"

Helena seemed to recognize the man. "You're that new arrival—Regin, isn't it?"

"Yes, ma'am. I rent rooms from Mala and her husband."

"And what business do you have with the Lady Sif?"

"It is with you, as well, ma'am," Regin said, "and with the rest of the council. You see, I know who the dragon is and where he comes from."

Sif had barely acknowledged the man up to this point, but now she turned to face him. "Then speak, and be quick about it! The more knowledge we have of this dragon, the easier it shall be to slay him."

"No!" Regin said a little too forcefully. Then he took a breath and got himself under control. "Apologies, milady, but I do not provide you with this intelligence to aid you in slaying Oter—but rather to save him."

Angrily, Helena said, "What possible reason could you have for wishing such a creature to be saved?"

"Because he is my brother."

CHAPTER FIVE

Night had fallen over Flodbjerge, and torches had been lit in the meeting hall. Sif and the members of the council had returned to their seats, and two more stools were brought in from the tavern—one for Regin and one for Hilde.

Bjorn and Olaf had both objected to Hilde's presence, as she was just a little girl, but before Sif could speak up to defend the honor of Volstagg's daughter, Frode had said, "Young Hilde is a bright and talented young woman. I believe she should be allowed to be part of this as much as Sif is."

Helena nodded. "Very well."

Hilde folded her arms and muttered, "Hmph."

Sif smiled. "Hilde did also find Regin here."

"Yes." Helena turned upon the gaunt man. "You said this dragon is your brother, and I must ask how this is even possible."

At that, Sif stared at Helena. "Two of Loki's sons are the Midgard Serpent and the Fenris Wolf. It is not as bizarre as you might think."

"And in fact," Regin said, "Oter once looked as you or I. But I get ahead of myself."

"Please do tell us of yourself and Oter," Sif said.

Helena added, "And explain why we should consider showing him mercy."

"Is not the fact that he is brother to one of your citizens enough?" Regin asked.

Olaf snorted. "You are barely a citizen of this town. In fact, had Helena not recognized you, I would have assumed you to be a stranger to us."

"It is true that I arrived comparatively recently, and it is also true that I keep to myself. But I would hope that the good people of Flodbjerge would not be cruel to a family member of one of its citizens."

"Several *other* of its citizens are now dead or injured because of said family member," Bjorn said, "so I would say you hope in vain."

"Nonetheless," Sif said quickly, "we know nothing of the dragon's motives and origins. Knowledge of such may affect how we approach the beast." Turning to Regin, she said, "Speak, Regin, and tell us of your brother."

"Oter and I were born in Nastrond, under the rule of the evil Fafnir. Our mother died when our younger brother was born—our brother, too, died soon thereafter."

"That's *awful*," Hilde said.

"It is, but I never knew either my mother or my brother, as Oter and I were both still very young when they died, so neither of us truly felt the sting of grief. Our father, however, was not so fortunate. He loved our mother dearly, and felt the pain of her loss every day." Regin shook his head. "However, we still needed to survive. Father was an expert hunter, and he trained Oter and I to hunt as well. In truth, however, his greatest skill was properly skinning the animals we captured to preserve their pelts. We would skin the animals, sell the meat to one of the butchers in Nastrond, and then sell the pelts. Our family gained a reputation as the purveyors of the finest pelts in the Nine Worlds."

Sif regarded Regin with renewed respect. "Tell me, Regin, is Hreidmar your father?"

Regin nodded. "Yes. You knew him?"

"By reputation only. The merchants from whom I have purchased furs for long winter journeys have always recommended the furs of Hreidmar because they are the finest."

"That pleases me greatly, milady. My father was truly an artist with a skinning knife."

"Yet you speak of him in the past tense."

"I am afraid so." Regin lowered his head. "As I am sure you are all aware, Nastrond was a most lawless place under Fafnir's rule. Bandits roamed the countryside, and one day, when we were on our way to the market in Gundersheim, we were beset by one."

"Only one?" Sif asked with surprise.

Bjorn turned to Sif. "Why does that surprise you?"

"In my experience, such roadside bandits travel in

numbers—it is difficult strategically for a single bandit to ambush a group. After all, if you wish to steal items from travelers, it is risky for one to remove valuables without having at least one other accomplice to hold weapons upon the victims."

"As it happens," Regin said, "the bandit who set upon us learned that lesson on this particular day. He attempted to make off with our pelts, but without that second person you mention, Lady Sif, he was unable to stop my father from attacking him in retaliation. But the bandit was armed as well, and his sword proved a more efficacious weapon than my father's skinning knife. So overcome with grief were we that we allowed the bandit to escape, as we were concerned only with being by our father's side for his final breath."

Helena pursed her lips. "I am so sorry."

Sif, though, said nothing, steeling herself instead for the next part of Regin's tale. Far too many stories of people transformed into creatures began with grief over a lost loved one.

Regin continued. "We brought our father back to Nastrond and performed a funeral for him. From that day forward, Oter and I swore we would track down that bandit and wreak revenge upon him for what he had done. For many months, we searched throughout Nastrond, Varinheim, and Gundersheim for the brigand who had taken our father from us."

Hilde, now literally sitting on the edge of her stool, was enraptured by Regin's story. "Did you find him?"

"Eventually, yes, Hilde, we did—but by the time we did so, we had spent all our coin. Our business was robust enough to keep us alive and fed when all three of us were active in its work, but after our father's death, my brother and I renounced the task of securing and selling pelts in favor of our quest for vengeance. By the time we were able to trace the brigand—to a cabin buried deep in the Norn Forest—all of our savings were gone. We were living off the land—cold, starving, miserable, with thoughts only of revenge."

"You must have loved your father a great deal," Hilde said.

"Yes," Regin said, "but it was more than that. We always aided our father and did what he told us. Without him, we had no guidance, no wisdom to lead us—we were the sons of Hreidmar and always did we do as he ordered. Vengeance was all we had left. And so it was a pair of thin, reedy, desperate, hungry men who approached that cabin in the Norn Forest."

"Was the brigand alone?" Sif asked.

Regin nodded. "And it was when we confronted him that we learned why—the cabin had only a pallet and no other furniture, for there was no room for it. All the rest of the space was filled with gold and jewels. Never had we seen the like. Oter and I were transfixed upon entering the cabin, and we lowered our swords and gaped.

"The bandit did stare at us. 'Who are you?' he asked.

"'I am Oter,' my brother said, 'and this is my brother, Regin. We have come to claim vengeance upon you, for you have slain our father, Hreidmar.'

"'I did?' The bandit seemed surprised.

"Angrily, I said, 'You set upon us on the road to Gundersheim and attempted to rob us. When our father tried to stop you, you did stab him!'

"The bandit shrugged. 'If that is what you do recall as occurring, I will not gainsay you. I have set upon many travelers on the road of which you speak, and I am sure that I have slain many such.'"

Sif frowned. "Did he not even put up a fight?"

"No, my lady, he did not. I hesitated, but Oter did not. He raised his sword and ran the man through without another thought."

Hilde shuddered.

Now Sif raised an eyebrow. "However, it would seem that your financial difficulties had come to an abrupt end."

Regin looked away. "After a fashion."

"Explain."

"We put as much of the gold and jewels as we could in our packs—including an emerald on a chain that the bandit wore around his neck. Our plan was to return to Nastrond and begin anew. The journey home was slow and arduous. Our plunder was quite heavy, and our horses were weak and feeble, for we were no more able to feed them than we were ourselves. As soon as we reached the village of Midluna, we immediately did purchase food and fresh mounts with our newly obtained gains.

"But soon, my brother and I did squabble. I wished only to return to our previous life, using enough of the bandit's gold to get our business started again, and putting the rest aside for use in our respective old ages. We were still young men, and the possibility of family was a real one.

"Oter, however, wanted none of that. 'We now have wealth beyond our wildest dreams, brother. Why put *any* of it aside? Why should we work and scrape and bow? What purpose is there in long days and nights in the forests and lakes in an attempt to capture game? What reason is there for us to travel throughout the Nine Worlds to market-places only to haggle with imbeciles who do not appreciate the value of our work? And why put money aside when the money is there for the taking?'"

"I take it he did not convince you?" Sif asked wryly.

"He did not. And so he stole away in the night—with the treasure and both our horses. He left only the emerald neck-lace, along with a note saying not to try to find him.

"Left with no recourse, and no coin save for an emer-ald that I doubted would feed me for more than a month, I returned to the bandit's cabin. I hoped that it was well pro-visioned, and at least I would have a place to sleep and eat while I determined what next to do, since my future plans had relied on the notion that I would have half the plunder.

"The day after my arrival, a dwarf smashed down the door. He had an axe raised over his head, but hesitated upon spying me in the sitting room. 'Who are you, and what have you done with Siegfried?'"

"I assume," Sif said, "that Siegfried was the bandit?"

Regin nodded. "I said to the dwarf, 'He is dead, his gold and jewels taken by a man named Oter.'

"The dwarf stared at the necklace around my neck. 'From whence did you obtain that necklace?'

"My sword was in another room, and the menace in the dwarf's tone made it clear that I should not prevaricate. 'From Siegfried. Oter is my brother, and he and I both sought revenge on him for our father's murder. But while I wished only for vengeance, Oter determined also to gain the wealth and prosperity of Siegfried's riches. And so he abandoned me, leaving only this emerald.'

"'Then your brother is a fool. That emerald is a charm that protects the wearer from all curses.'

"This surprised me, but also pleased me, obviously—for being immune to curses was a state of affairs I found to be advantageous. 'No doubt,' I said, 'Siegfried used it to protect himself from anything he might have stolen that was cursed.'

"'You speak true, stranger,' the dwarf said, 'for the gold he stole from the dwarves was so cursed.'"

Sif shook her head. "The dwarf also spoke true when he named your brother a fool. Those who steal from the dwarves quickly learn to regret it."

"Indeed." Regin sighed. "The dwarf did, at least, spare my life, satisfied as he was that Siegfried was dead—though he did take the emerald from me."

"A pity," Bjorn said.

With a glower at Bjorn, Sif said, "Hardly. Charms to fend off curses are but stopgaps, and tend only to cause the curse to seek its foulness elsewhere." She turned to Regin. "I assume the dwarf explained that the curse of this particular gold was to turn any who hoarded it into a dragon?"

"Yes, milady."

Olaf asked, "How came you here to Flodbjerge?"

"By the time I returned to Nastrond, there was nothing of it left. Even the river was fused to a faceted crystal."

Quietly, Sif said, "The wrath of Odin. Fafnir did rule in Nastrond, and so vile was he that all who had goodness in their hearts were driven from the land. Those who remained were amongst the foulest beings who ever populated the Nine Worlds, and Odin did destroy them all."

"I know not of that, milady," Regin said, "but I do know that I had no home to return to. So I did wander the Realm Eternal, finding what work I could with my skills as a hunter. Eventually, I amassed enough coin to settle in a new place, far from my old life."

"And you happened to come here?" Sif asked. "To the very place where your brother has hoarded his cursed gold?"

"I know not how Oter found himself in the Valhalla Mountains, Lady Sif, but I do know that it is the first time I have encountered my brother since he left me in Midluna. And I wish to save him from this awful fate. He has suffered enough, trapped by the gold and the desire to hoard the treasure but never spend it. That, you see, is the true curse of the dwarves. A dragon may only protect his hoard, and perhaps add to it, but the protection of it becomes all."

Sif rubbed her chin thoughtfully. "No doubt he believes you to be a threat to his hoard, as you claimed it together, and so he has been attacking Flodbjerge to eliminate that threat."

"No doubt." Regin nodded.

"It also explains why he attacks in the manner he does."

"How so?" Olaf asked, confused.

Sif stared intently at Olaf. "Curses are extremely powerful. If Oter is compelled to protect the hoard, he cannot be away from it for very long. So his attacks last only as long as he may stay away from his treasure."

Helena hopped off the tavern stool. "Revealing though all this may be, it is of no relevance."

Regin's eyes grew wide. "How can you say that?"

"I am truly heartbroken over what has happened to you and your brother, Regin. To lose a father is a terrible burden.

But the responsibility of this council is to safeguard the village. In order to do so, Oter *must* be killed—and quickly, before more of Flodbjerge is leveled, and more of its citizenry killed or injured."

Bjorn shook his head. "If Oter is looking for his brother, why not simply give him what he seeks?"

Regin blanched.

Helena turned upon Bjorn. "No. I will not sacrifice any more of Flodbjerge's denizens to this dragon."

"He's barely one of us!" Bjorn cried.

Shaking her head, Helena said, "That matters not. Besides, there is no guarantee that giving Regin to Oter would even stop the dragon."

"However," Sif said in a hard voice, "there *is* a guarantee that if you commit so craven an act as to give Regin over, you will divest yourself of my protection—and that of any of Asgard's warriors henceforth."

Quickly, Bjorn said, "I meant no disrespect, Lady Sif; I simply wished to consider all the options."

"Then let me provide you with another option," Regin said urgently. "The curse may be removed."

That got Sif's attention. "You might have stated that earlier, Regin. Tell us how, quickly!"

"Oter must be defeated in combat at his lair, and then physically removed from his hoard. Only then may the curse be lifted."

Olaf nodded. "There is only one thing for it. Milady, you must send your girl here to Asgard to fetch Thor."

Sif whirled on Olaf with fury behind her eyes. "I beg your pardon?"

Hilde jumped off her stool. "I don't have to go to Asgard for anything, because Sif can win in *any* fight—even with a big, stupid dragon!"

After throwing a small smile at Hilde, Sif turned back to Olaf. "For millennia, the greatest foes I have faced are fools such as you, who would use gender as a criterion for determining a warrior's heart. Be assured, Olaf, that I have fought many foes for many decades, and none have yet earned the title of 'Killer of Sif.'"

Holding up both hands, Olaf said, "Please, milady, do not misunderstand me. I hold you in the highest regard."

"Save, perhaps, with regard to my height," Sif said wryly.

"Indeed, Lady Sif, I expected greater height from you precisely because the tales of your prowess are so impressive. But it is not your gender that I find lacking. Were Balder the Brave present in your place, or any of the Warriors Three, or Harokin, of the Einherjar, my response would be the same. Thor is the God of Thunder, the son of Odin. Save for the All-Father himself, there is none mightier in the Nine Worlds. And he has slain dragons before."

Sif smiled. "And you think I have not?" The smile fell. "Regardless, Olaf, even if I acceded to your request, it would not be possible for Hilde or me to fulfill it. The God of Thunder is abed, and the healers have urged him to remain so for many more weeks. Thor did do battle against Hrungnir of the Frost Giants, and while the giant was defeated, Thor's victory came at a great price. As Helena said, time is of the essence, and we cannot wait for Thor's recovery to ask him to take on the dragon—nor is such a query required."

"As I said, milady, I meant no disrespect to your abilities as a warrior." Olaf sounded nervous now. "I merely point out that you are not Thor."

"And Thor is not Sif. Remember that, Olaf, and remember that the path of my life is littered with the corpses of those who thought me weaker or lesser than the men around me."

Before Olaf could even consider formulating a response, a man ran into the hall.

"The dragon returns!"

Helena's eyes grew wide. "Never has the interval between attacks been so short."

Frode frowned. "The last attack was shorter than the others—perhaps that is why?"

Shaking her head, Sif said, "The reasons matter not. Oter will find Flodbjerge to be far better defended than it was in the past!" She pointed at Regin. "Hide him in the most secure location you have in this village. Do all that is possible to deny Oter his prize."

"And what will you do?" Regin asked.

Sif unsheathed her sword. "End this madness once and for all!"

CHAPTER SIX

Sif ran out into the thoroughfares of Flodbjerge, sword at
the ready. Looking up into the sky, she saw Oter heading
for the houses alongside the river in the southwestern portion of the village—exactly where she had expected him to
strike next.

Angry that they had not had a chance to remove the
items from the repair shop, Sif revised her opinion of
Frode's earlier remarks. Perhaps Sif's resistance *had* caused
Oter to leave Flodbjerge sooner than he had planned. She
had wounded him, after all, which was more than had happened to him on any of his other attacks.

The dragon was swooping downward, toward the large
structure that had to be the repair shop. But he was still quite
distant, having just come out of the mountains. Gritting her
teeth, Sif ran toward the shop, hoping that she would be able
to reach it before the dragon's arrival.

Her feet carried her well, for she did indeed arrive ahead of
the dragon. She held her sword aloft and said, "Ho, dragon!
Be gone from this place! You will not find your brother here,
and if you do any more harm to the good people of this village, you will face the wrath of Sif!"

The creature swooped over the repair shop, then flew up and around, making a loop in the air. He stopped, hovering over the shop, and Sif was able to get a better look at the dragon than she had before, lit as he was by the torches along the Gopul River and by the dragon's own maw, which smoldered and glowed. While Oter's wingspan was impressive, Sif realized that it created the illusion that the dragon was larger than he truly was. In fact, his body was only about twice the size of that of Sif herself, though his wings unfurled to twice *that* length again.

The dragon spoke, and Oter's voice rumbled as though shuddering forward from the very earth itself. "The wrath of Sif? Am I to be impressed by this declaration? Who are you, little girl, whose wrath claims to be sufficient to challenge Oter the dragon?"

"I am Sif! I am she who has done battle against the Frost Giants of Jotunheim and the minions of Surtur! I have fought alongside Thor the Thunderer and Beta Ray Bill! I have faced gods and villains! I am a warrior and a goddess, and you are a failed peddler of pelts who has been granted delusions of menace by a dwarf's curse!"

"And are only words to defeat me this day? You claim to be a goddess, and claim also to know the man I was. But all I see is a little girl who speaks words that mean nothing. No man has ever defeated me in battle, and I highly doubt that a woman will do so now."

"Flodbjerge is under my protection, dragon. Return to your hoard and cease your search for your sibling."

"And if I refuse, little girl?"

Now Sif grinned. "Oh, I sincerely hope that you do, Oter, for I will take great pleasure in ending your reign in a much bloodier manner."

The dragon chuckled, smoke bursting forth from his maw. "You risk much, little girl."

Raising her sword, Sif cried, "Choose, dragon! Return to your hoard and live your life in peace, or stay and end your life in battle!"

Oter did not answer with words, but instead dove straight for Sif.

Sif also dove, rolling away from the dragon's attack. Oter arced back upward.

To Sif's relief, the dragon didn't actually attack the repair shop. Whatever else Sif calling him out had accomplished, it served well the purpose of focusing Oter's wrath on her rather than on his devastating search for his brother.

Getting to her feet, Sif sheathed her sword, then ran toward another nearby structure and leapt to its roof, her powerful legs easily propelling her upward. As soon as her feet gained purchase, she ran to the far edge of the roof.

Oter was flying back down toward the same building onto which she'd leapt, making Sif's plan that much easier to enact.

The dragon opened his maw, preparing to use his fiery exhalation on Sif, but she leapt into the air, a running start giving her even greater distance than her jump from the ground had.

Flying through the air, she reached out to gain purchase upon one of the dragon's talons. In addition to his wings, the creature had four short legs on the underside of his body that ended in three sharp talons each, and Sif managed to snag a talon on one of the forelegs.

Screaming, Oter flew upward, then quickly bucked left and right in an attempt to dislodge Sif.

Any hope she had to stab the dragon was dashed, as Oter's movements made it incredibly difficult for Sif to maintain her hold upon the creature's talons with even two hands. A one-handed grip would be insufficient, and she would plummet to the ground or the river.

The dragon continued to change directions in ever-more chaotic maneuvers, trying to dislodge Sif, but she would not let go.

So Oter altered his strategy. He flew straight upward into the dark night sky, as fast as his lengthy wings would carry him.

One of the things that made Thor stand out from his fellow Asgardians was the gift of flight granted him by his Uru hammer, Mjolnir; even Odin had not the ability to carry himself through the air.

SIF: Even Dragons Have Their Endings

On Midgard, Sif had encountered many of Thor's colleagues, dubbed "superheroes" by the mortals, who could fly through the air unaided. Sif had even fought alongside some of them.

On those occasions when someone had carried her while using their power of flight, Sif had always found it exhilarating. She thrilled at how the wind moving past her could be experienced by all five of her senses at once—the feel of it pressing against her body and running through her hair, the sight of it filtering through the tears it caused in her eyes, the sound of it as it roared in her ears, the smell of her sweat, instantly evaporated by it, and the taste of it on her tongue even as it dried her mouth.

None of that exhilaration was present now as Oter streaked ever upward, rising nearly to the peaks of the Valhalla Mountains.

But still she held on.

The wind didn't just press against her body as she clung to the dragon's talon, it pounded her. Her eyes were forced shut by the intensity of the flight, and the roar of the wind nearly deafened her. The only smell her nose could detect was the fetid stench of Oter's fiery breath, and her throat had gone so dry, she could taste nothing.

But still she held on.

Then Oter ceased his upward motion. The dragon hung in the air for but a second, yet to Sif it seemed much longer;

they were poised so high that when she briefly opened her eyes, the village of Flodbjerge was but a speck on the ground beneath her.

Oter craned his neck downward, and suddenly, both dragon and his unexpected passenger plummeted. With each second they went faster, accelerating toward the Gopul River.

But still she held on.

She had to use both arms and both legs, but Sif did still clutch to the dragon's talon, refusing to give in. He could not harm her directly, as it was impossible for him to crane his head to his underside in such a way for his breath to be effective—even were he willing to immolate his own limb. And his talons were stunted and far apart, each unable to reach any of the others.

Left without those two options, Oter was forced to try to shake Sif off.

As he descended toward the Gopul, he angled himself so that he would not enter the water directly, but would instead skim its surface with his belly.

The dragon's underside, including his talons and the Lady Sif, hit the water with sufficient force that it was akin to striking a stone wall.

But still she held on.

Battered, bruised, bloody, soaked to her very bones, Sif refused to loosen her grip even as Oter once again flew up into the air.

The dragon hovered for a moment. "Still you vex me, little girl!"

That hesitation, and expression of annoyance, was all Sif required to let go of the talon with one hand, unsheathe her sword, and run it into the dragon's underside.

Oter's scream filled the heavens with fire as he reared back his head, crying and thrashing about in agony.

With only one hand gripped upon the talon, Oter's thrashing managed what could not be done before, and Sif lost her hold.

The dragon still hovered over the Gopul, so Sif straightened her body and dove into the river.

This plunge into the cold waters of the Gopul was far kinder than the previous one had been, and she surfaced after only a moment.

Oter stopped his cries of pain long enough to peer down at Sif. "You will rue the day you challenged me, little girl!"

Sheathing her sword while treading water, Sif said, "You will rue the day you called me 'little girl.'"

The dragon dove downward at Sif, so she submerged herself once again, swimming underwater toward the shore.

Even as she swam below the water—her strong legs propelling her, her capacious lungs allowing her to hold her breath—Oter breathed fire at the river. But while Sif could feel the heat of the flames, and they no doubt turned the water's surface to steam, she was deep enough to remain unharmed.

Upon reaching the shore, she clambered out of the water and unsheathed her sword.

Oter hovered over the river, glowering at her with his watery, yellow eyes. His voice rumbled even louder now. "You vex me, little girl, and you will die at my hand!"

"Unlikely." Sif ran downriver, away from the town, hoping that Oter would follow.

That hope was fulfilled, as the dragon flew after her, catching up to her as she reached the southernmost part of the town and the abandoned boathouse she had noticed on their way in.

Sif ran into the boathouse, then immediately ran out the other side, out of sight of the dragon.

As she'd hoped, Oter headed straight for the boathouse itself, coming to a halt just outside it, and exhaling heavily upon it.

The dilapidated wooden structure immediately caught fire, but Sif was already far enough away from it to be unharmed, having run outside and doubled around.

Oter raised his head and cackled—a low, rumbling sound that seemed to shake the very sky.

"Burn, little girl, burn! None may challenge Oter and live! Not that fool Siegfried, not my idiot brother, not the dwarves, and not our f—AAAARRRRRGGGGGGHHH!"

That last cry came as Sif leapt onto the dragon's back and plunged her sword into his scaly hide.

Oter flew back and forth, writhing in agony. Sif, with no talons to grip, fell to the ground, but managed to roll onto her right shoulder as she landed, dulling the impact.

As she got to her feet, Sif paused a moment to catch her breath. She ignored the fact that her entire body felt like one big bruise.

Oter thrashed about in the air. Sif's sword still protruded from his back, and the dragon was helpless to remove it. His tail hit the river hard, violently splashing water all about, including onto the engulfed boathouse.

Looking down at Sif, his yellow eyes now murderous, Oter screamed in a voice that shook the very foundations of Flodbjerge.

"You *will* die for this, little girl!"

"Many have made that claim, including other dragons far fiercer than you, Oter, yet Sif remains—and they are all dust."

"As will you be shortly."

But before the dragon could make good on his threat, he was pelted by debris—tools, rotten food, and other detritus flew threw the air, striking the dragon's hide.

Both Sif and her foe turned toward the source of the impromptu missiles.

A group of villagers had gathered nearby, and at the forefront of them was Hilde.

"Get away from here, dragon!" cried the daughter of

Volstagg. "We're sick of you, and we don't want you here!" She punctuated her outburst by heaving a rock the size of her hand.

The rock flew through the air and slammed into the dragon's neck. It was followed quickly by a broken rake, a few more stones, and rotten fish (the stench of which, after a moment, reached Sif's nose).

Oter screamed, flames bursting from his mouth and into the night air.

And then the dragon turned and flew toward the mountains, Sif's sword still jutting from his back.

Sif watched in fury as the creature flew away, and then turned in surprise at the sudden sound of the villagers cheering.

Slowly, she walked over to the villagers, the water from her two trips into the Gopul making her armor squeak as she moved. Several of the villagers had already broken off, led by Frode, and were moving to put out the boathouse fire before it could spread. At least the dragon's splashing tail had made that job easier.

"Wasn't that great?" Hilde asked, a big grin on her face.

But Sif only glared at the girl. "Hardly. The fight was not yet finished!"

"It is now," Helena said.

Sif turned on the leader of the council. "Twice did I strike a blow against the dragon, but before I could even consider a third, you drove him off! And he still has my sword! You interfered in a battle that was not yet complete!"

Helena merely stood with her arms folded. "Milady, every time the dragon has attacked, there have been deaths and the destruction of valuable property. Until tonight. Tonight, no one died, and the only damage was to a boathouse that was already half fallen to ruin."

"Besides," Hilde said, "Regin said you had to defeat the dragon and take him away from his hoard to turn him back into a person again. Can't do that if you defeat him *here*. You have to find his hoard."

Helena added, "Which is preferable to another pitched battle against a creature who breathes fire within the confines of Flodbjerge. Or would you have the dragon destroy what few structures are still left standing before you defeat him?"

Sif's retort died on her lips. She could argue with neither of them. Well, in truth, she *could*—but the arguments all boiled down to her desire to continue the fight regardless of the consequences.

Turning to look at Frode and the others using buckets to scoop water from the Gopul to extinguish the boathouse fire, Sif was reminded that the consequences of continued battle could be dire indeed.

"Very well. I will track the dragon to his lair."

With that, Sif moved off, determined to end this.

CHAPTER SEVEN

Volstagg was late arriving home.

He had intended to come straight back to the house after visiting with Thor, but he had been sidetracked by the fruit merchant, who had had some wonderful pears and persimmons for Volstagg to sample. And then, he had been distracted by the stew being cooked inside one of the inns on the main road, which he of course needed to taste to make sure it was up to the cook's usual standards. And then, he had been waylaid by some young people who wanted to hear tales of Volstagg's bravery, and who was he to deny his public?

When Volstagg did arrive home, he saw several of his children playing. He observed that the very youngest were nowhere to be found—which was well, as they were supposed to be in bed by now.

The older children were playing games together, or reading books from the library, or munching on some dessert or other that Volstagg intended to sample to make sure it was of adequate quality for his offspring to consume.

As he did the latter, he noticed that Alaric and Hilde were conspicuous by their absences. They were not of a temperament to go to bed early—indeed, there were some nights when Volstagg feared he would need to strap them to their beds to get them there by the witching hour.

After sampling the desserts, and leaving at least a little bit for the children, Volstagg regarded his wife Gudrun, asleep on the couch.

For a moment he smiled, enjoying the peaceful sight of his lovely wife, lying on her side, arms wrapped around a throw pillow. Times like these reminded Volstagg why he had married her.

Then one eye opened. Gudrun spied Volstagg, and shot upward. "Where have you *been*?" she said in a scratchy, scolding tone—made worse by the dryness of her mouth upon waking.

"I—"

"*Don't* give me excuses! The children have been simply *awful* most of the day, and where were you? Hm?"

"Well, I—"

"And the worst part is that Hilde and Alaric got into a fight!"

That brought Volstagg up short. "What about?"

"I have absolutely no idea. It was something about one of your hunting knives—the one you're having repaired."

"Why were they—"

"And another thing—dinner was absolutely ruined because you were supposed to be home for it, and I had to waste all the extra food I cooked because I thought you were to be here."

"I—"

"So what do you have to say for yourself? Well? Answer me! Why will you not speak?"

Conversations like this reminded Volstagg why he so often went on adventures.

"I assume," he finally said, "that you confined Alaric and Hilde to their rooms?"

"Of course! They know the punishment for roughhousing. I do not approve of such behavior in this house from *anyone*."

Volstagg nodded. "I will speak to them."

As he moved toward the back of the house, which contained all of the children's bedrooms, Gudrun called out, "We are not finished discussing dinner!"

"Of that I have no doubt," Volstagg muttered.

Vaguely, he remembered that Alaric had used the dragon-hilt hunting knife in a ridiculous attempt to cut down the hardwood tree on the lawn.

As he approached Alaric's room, Volstagg recalled that he had long ago promised that knife to Hilde. In truth, he offered many items to his children, not expecting them to recall the conversation the next day, much less years later. Hilde had been just a small child when she'd taken an interest in the dragon-hilt knife, and Volstagg had not yet learned what a special girl his daughter was to become. He had promised her the knife, thinking nothing would come of it.

The fight that had ensued this day indicated that something had come of it, and far sooner than Volstagg would have expected, even if he had intended to gift the knife to Hilde.

Opening the door, he saw Alaric lying on his bed—he shared the room with several of his brothers, but the other boys were playing games or eating dessert elsewhere in the house—in very much the same position Gudrun had been in on the couch.

However, Volstagg's mien was not melted by Alaric's angelic visage, as it had been by Gudrun's—partly because he was upset at his son, and partly because the boy himself had a frown on his face as he clutched his pillow to him.

As soon as Volstagg entered, Alaric sat up. "It's not my fault!" he cried out without preamble.

With a smile, Volstagg said, "You do not even know the purpose of my entering."

"Yes, I do. Mother told you to yell at me for getting into a fight with Hilde, but *she* started it!"

"Tell me precisely what transpired, my son." Volstagg took a seat at the foot of Alaric's bed. The springs groaned from the weight of the Lion of Asgard's corpulent form.

"I was just *sitting* in the living room! All of a sudden, Hilde comes out of *nowhere* and asks about *her* knife. I didn't think she *had* a knife, and I *said* so! She said the dragon-hilt knife, which I thought was *your* knife that you used against the Fenris Wolf. And then she *hit* me!"

"Did you explain to Hilde why the knife in question was not on the shelf?"

Alaric squirmed a bit. "Well, yeah."

"Hilde spoke the truth," Volstagg said, patting his son on the knee. "I did promise that knife to her when she became old enough to wield it properly. Be grateful that today is not that day, for she might have used it on you."

Frowning, Alaric asked, "How could she if it's being repaired?"

"Never mind that," Volstagg said quickly. "The point is, you took something that wasn't yours."

"But you already punished me for that! That's not fair!"

Volstagg shook his head. "Ah, my son, it is important that you know that, despite the best efforts of parents to protect their children from this awful truth, the fact of the matter is that life is almost never fair. And a life as long as we Aesir live means that such unfairness comes in even greater quantity." Again, he patted his son on the knee, and then said, "Now then, go to sleep. Tomorrow, I expect three apologies from you, and they are to be heartfelt."

"Three?" Alaric's voice squeaked. "Why three?"

"One to your mother for putting up with your nonsense, one to Hilde for taking her knife, and one to me for using that knife in a manner that is, quite frankly, appalling. A hardwood tree, really, son?"

"I'm sorry, Fath—"

Volstagg held up one finger. "No! The apologies must be proffered publicly to the entire household come morning."

"Do I have to?"

"Rest assured that you will receive one apology in exchange from Hilde, also in front of the entire household."

Alaric grinned at that. "Good."

After tucking his son into bed, Volstagg left the room and went to the room shared by the girls. To his consternation, however, he saw only the youngest girl, Flosi, asleep in her bed.

Hilde's bed was neatly made and completely unslept in.

To be sure, he checked the wardrobe—Hilde would sometimes hide therein, though that had been mostly when she was much younger.

But it only had the girls' clothes in it.

"Father?" came Flosi's bleary voice from her bed.

"Have you seen your sister, Flosi?"

"You mean Hilde? Nuh-uh, she wasn't here when I came to bed."

With a heavy sigh, Volstagg patted his little girl on the head. "Thank you, Flosi. Go back to sleep now."

"Okay," she said through a yawn, and fell back to sleep almost instantly.

Quickly, Volstagg returned to the front of the house.

"Hilde is not in her room."

Gudrun had gotten up from the couch and was now in the kitchen cleaning up the dishes, one of which, at her husband's words, she dropped. "What!?"

"My dear, I am sorry, but Hilde is not in her room, and Flosi says that Hilde wasn't there when she went to bed."

Letting out a moan of anguish, Gudrun dropped another plate onto the floor.

Volstagg quickly led Gudrun out of the kitchen and back to the living room, lest she destroy all their crockery. "Hrolf!" he called out to one of his sons. "Clean up the mess in the kitchen, please!"

"Yes, Father!"

Volstagg sat Gudrun down on the couch and said, "Worry not, my dear love, for the Lion of Asgard will not allow any harm to befall our daughter. I will go immediately to Heimdall and ask if his all-seeing vision has spied Hilde. If he has, I will follow his directions as to where to fetch her. If he has not, then I will leave no stone in any of the Nine Worlds unturned until I have found her! So speaks Volstagg!"

CHAPTER EIGHT

Having spent the remainder of the evening before going over maps of the area that had been provided by the Flodbjerge council, Sif waited until morning to begin her journey up the mountain. While no one was sure precisely where in the mountains Oter was keeping his hoard, Sif did poll the villagers to get at least a general idea of the vicinity where it was likely to be.

"The difficulty," Frode had said to her after they had discussed the matter, "is that when the dragon departs, we are far more concerned with assessing the damage to both people and property to pay significant attention to his destination. As well, that damage, as we said, is accompanied by a great deal of smoke. Oter seldom approaches from the same direction, and we rarely see him until he is almost upon us."

However, they had been able to narrow down Oter's destination to at least a section of the mountains—one that Bjorn had assured her had plenty of caves in which the dragon could hide himself and his pile of gold and jewels.

At first light, Sif provisioned herself with jerky provided by Olaf and his wife, and took her leave.

"I still think," Olaf said, "that Frode should've brought Thor."

His wife smacked his arm. "Hush, Olaf. Sif drove off the dragon single handedly last night and hardly broke anything in the process. Remember when we were visiting your mother in Varinheim while those Storm Giants were trying to invade, and Thor stopped them? He made a total mess! Throwing that hammer all around, knocking things over, all that lightning. Just awful. This lady knows how to fight in a civilized manner."

Sif smiled and bowed her head to Olaf's wife. "Thank you, my lady. I will endeavor to minimize the collateral damage to your fine village."

Bjorn came up to her, holding out a longsword in a scabbard. "It's not much, milady, but I thought you might prefer not to engage the creature unarmed. It belonged to my father, and he used it in battle on Midgard alongside Thor, defending the mortals there."

On the one hand, Sif was grateful, as it was always better to do battle with a good sword in your hand than without. On the other hand, she had no idea whether this was a good sword—especially if it hadn't been used in a millennium.

But then Bjorn unsheathed the sword, and Sif saw that it was sharp and gleaming. He said, "I have cared for it well. Every morning when I awaken, I sharpen it. Every evening before I sleep, I polish it."

Bjorn handed Sif the sword, and upon wrapping her

hand around the hilt, she knew immediately that it was a well-balanced weapon—heavy enough to be strong, but light enough to be swung.

"My father named the sword Gunnvarr," Bjorn added.

Sif held it upraised in a salute. "I thank you for the loan of Gunnvarr, and pray that it tastes Oter's blood ere long."

Bjorn bowed. "You're very welcome, milady."

Sif's next stop was to fill her canteen from the Gopul River. It would be at least a day's walk up the mountain, and she hoped that the dragon would be compelled to remain by his hoard for at least that duration, wounded as he had been by Sif's sword.

As the river water flowed into her canteen, she heard the light tread of a child approaching. Without turning around, Sif asked, "What is it, Hilde?"

"How—?" Hilde sighed loudly. "Never mind. I want to come with you."

Sif rose and turned to face the girl. "Hilde . . ."

Volstagg's daughter held up both hands. "Look, I don't want to *face* the dragon again—I don't think throwing things at him will work a second time—but I want to at least help *track* him. Once we get into the mountains, he'll need to be tracked, right? You taught me all those skills, and I want to use them!"

"Hilde, it will be a difficult path to traverse."

"It's just mountains. When Mother and Frigga took us

through the Asgard Mountains when the giants attacked, we were fine. And these mountains aren't as high, or as snowy!"

Sif sighed. The desire to keep the daughter of the Voluminous One safe warred with Sif's lack of desire to leave Hilde alone in the village to cause mischief unsupervised. The people of Flodbjerge had enough to worry about.

"Unless you don't think I'm good enough," Hilde added.

Sif winced. Not long after her lessons with Tyr had ceased, she, Thor, and Fandral had learned of an imminent attack upon Vanaheim by a contingent of trolls. Odin had asked Thor and Fandral to come along, along with two others who'd been part of Tyr's lessons—but not Sif.

Sif's response to the All-Father then had been, "Am I not good enough?"

Odin had relented then, and Sif felt compelled to do so now. Besides, if nothing else, the company would be pleasant. Slowly, she said, "It might be useful to see how much you truly learned during the week we spent together. It is far easier to enact lessons learned the same day—the true test is if those lessons are retained after time."

Hilde jumped up and down and raised her arms. "Yay!"

They walked back into town, Sif placing her canteen in her pack.

Regin approached them from the council hall. "Helena informs me that you wish to speak with me, milady."

"Yes, Regin. It is possible that Oter will come down from the mountain while I—" Sif looked down at Hilde. "While *we* are searching for him. Therefore, it is imperative that you hide yourself. I recommend that you hide in the storehouse. Your brother already knows it is a place you are not likely to be."

"That is very sensible, milady, thank you."

"Be warned," she added quickly, "that the place is kept cold by magic that preserves its piscine stores."

Regin smiled. "Our family's hunts took us to the northern regions of Nastrond, and often into Niffleheim itself. Many is the night I spent in tents during the fiercest blizzards that the northern realms could offer. Cold and sleep are old friends of mine."

Sif put an encouraging hand on his shoulder. "Excellent. I will do what I can to save your brother from his curse—but know that I will put the safety of these good people over that of a man who leaves his brother abandoned and penniless."

"I do understand, milady. I ask only that if the opportunity for mercy presents itself, you do take it. I would very much like my brother back—but I also fear that he has been lost to me ever since he left with the cursed gold."

Sif nodded, and then set off, Hilde right behind her.

* * *

The initial travel proved difficult. The Valhalla Mountains, though shorter than Asgard's mountains, were much steeper at the base.

After spending the better part of the morning clambering up a sheer rock face, Sif and Hilde found a natural pathway up and around one of the mountains that took them on a more pleasant, if still difficult, path.

At one point, Hilde muttered, "The Asgard Mountains had far more straight passages than this."

Sif chuckled. "The Asgard Mountains have had many more travelers upon them, situated between Asgard and Jotunheim; they are a much-trod-upon path. By contrast, these mountains see far less foot traffic. No doubt that is part of why Oter chose them as the place to hoard his ill-gotten wealth."

Eventually, they paused to eat the jerky and drink the water, to regain their strength after the first part of their journey.

"Tell a story, Sif?" Hilde asked.

In truth, Sif would have preferred to eat in peace, but Hilde seemed so insistent and enthusiastic at the notion. "Be warned, I am not the storyteller your father is."

"It's okay—nobody tells stories like *he* does. But I want to hear about one of *your* adventures."

"Shall I tell you of the time Thor and I fought the Midgard vampire known as Dracula? Or when brave Balder and I faced the Enchanters? Or when Beta Ray Bill and I fought the demons who menaced his home world? Or when I joined the Avengers in battle against mutants in the Savage Land? Or when your father, Fandral, Hogun, and I did—"

"No, I want to hear about an adventure that's *just you*. Not when you're helping out one of the other warriors of Asgard—an adventure of *Sif*."

"Very well." Sif leaned back against a rock. "Balder and I faced the Enchanters in the realm of Ringsfjord. Foul sorcerers, were they—three who possessed the Living Talismans, and therefore power to rival that of the All-Father himself. Originally, Odin did instruct only Balder to go to Ringsfjord to gain intelligence regarding the Enchanters and their plan to attack Asgard, but I spoke of my own time spent in Ringsfjord, and so Odin did grant me leave to accompany Balder on his journey."

"I thought you weren't going to tell that story."

"I am not; I merely mention our mission as a prelude to the story I *am* to tell." Sif took a bite of her jerky, washing it down with the water from her canteen before continuing. "My previous trip to Ringsfjord that gained me that familiarity came during the time of Thor's exile on Midgard, when he was trapped in the body of a lame mortal healer named Donald Blake. But the blink of an eye in Asgard, it *seemed* an eternity to those of us who love Thor—for to be without the thunder god's companionship for so long was difficult."

Hilde grinned. "Companionship? Is that what you grownups call that?"

Sif glowered at the girl. "My relationship with Thor is *not* the subject of this story, Hildegard."

"Father says that—"

"We shall not discuss Volstagg's gossip, either," Sif said sternly. "You wished to hear the story of my first journey to Ringsfjord, and Thor is only a part of it, insofar as his absence prompted the journey." She shook her head ruefully. "After a fashion."

"What do you mean?"

"There was a couple of my acquaintance who lived in Asgard. The boy was the son of the stable master, and the girl was the daughter of the seamstress royal. They grew up together, and the stable master and the seamstress did promise the two of them to each other."

Hilde wrinkled her nose. "Okay."

"You do not approve?"

"I don't want to marry *anyone*! And if I do, it'll be someone *I* want, not someone chosen by my parents."

Grinning, Sif said, "I doubt Hogun will ever wish to marry, Hilde."

Hilde turned away and blushed. Her crush on Hogun was the worst-kept secret in the Realm Eternal.

"In any event, Hilde, not all are so fortunate as to indulge their own wishes. Look at the All-Father and Frigga."

"What about them? They're the best couple in Asgard!"

"And theirs was an arranged marriage, just as that of

these two children was to be. Odin and Frigga did marry to unite Asgard and Vanaheim."

Hilde blinked. "I didn't know that."

"The daughter of the seamstress felt much as you do. She was fond of the boy, but had no wish to spend the rest of her life with him. However, she couldn't bear to disappoint her mother, and so she concocted a plan. In Ringsfjord there is a great stone known as the Eye of Gerda. It is one of the finest jewels in all the Nine Worlds, and it is guarded by two trolls, who take turns watching it. One guards while the other sleeps. The troll on guard holds a weapon known as Sigivald—a club that guarantees victory to its wielder.

"The girl told the boy that her most fervent desire was for him to give her the Eye of Gerda as a wedding present. She believed that he would go on his own to obtain the jewel, and then be defeated by the troll. Since the troll's weapon was only a club, she believed that the boy would not be unduly harmed, and that he would return to Asgard injured but alive—and unwilling to marry her for the shame of his failure."

"And instead, he sent you?" Hilde guessed.

Sif nodded. "I did owe the boy, for he had nursed my mare back to health after she was injured during a battle against the Storm Giants. I had thought the mount to be lost forever, and she was the finest horse that ever I did ride. When he presented my mare to me, ready to charge into battle once again, I did tell him that I would perform any favor he asked."

"It was mean of him to ask you."

Sif shrugged. "It was practical. For while the girl had only simple sisterly affection for the boy, he was utterly devoted to her. Neither he nor I knew of Sigivald, only that the Eye of Gerda was guarded by a troll armed only with a club. The boy was no fighter—he barely knew which end of the sword to hold, much less how to wield one."

"That's not really even, is it? I mean, he just nursed a horse. You had to fight a troll!"

"It is not a question, Hilde, of scale, but of ability. It is not within my power to return a horse to a healthy state after an injury, but it is within his. It is not within his power to do battle with a troll, but it is within mine.

"And so I set forth on the very mare that the boy had healed. This was not long after Odin had exiled Thor to Midgard—to teach him humility, or so the All-Father said—and I was feeling his loss keenly. The distraction of a quest was very welcome, and so I did ride into Ringsfjord.

"The terrain there is difficult, as the ground is subject to quakes and tremors. It is made almost entirely of rock, and I have been told by others that it is a great source of magic—which is why the Enchanters did later use it as their base of operations. However, I was able to work my way through, dodging falling rocks and navigating uneven stone passages before finding my way to the troll.

"The troll did not speak, but stared mutely ahead. I did challenge him verbally, but he said not a word.

"'I wish to take the Eye of Gerda!' I cried, but the troll still simply stared.

"Until, that is, I came within a hand's length of him, and then he swung Sigivald with a speed that belied his massive form. Barely was I able to dodge the attack, and I did immediately strike back.

"But no matter what strike I used, no matter how fast or agile I was, always did the troll parry my attack. One moment the club was over his head defending my downward strike, then it somehow was there to deflect my foot when I kicked the troll only a moment past. It seemed impossible, and quickly I deduced that sorcery had to be involved. Magic is an art of the mind, and trolls are not known for swiftness in that particular organ, so I doubted that the sorcery came from the creature himself, or from his sleeping companion. It therefore had to be the weapon.

"And so I did focus my attack not on the troll's head or heart—for the wisest course of action when attempting to disable or kill a foe is to strike at one of those portions of the body—but instead on the creature's right arm. Always was the club held in that arm, never once switching. That, too, bespoke enchantment, for several times I attacked in such a manner that switching hands would have been efficacious, but the blinding speed with which the troll parried made that unnecessary.

"After trading a few blows, I made several attempts to attack his right arm, but he proved as skilled at blocking those as he had all the others."

Hilde was now on the edge of the rock on which she'd been sitting. "So how did you win?"

"I retreated briefly to consider my options. As I suspected, once I moved a certain distance from the troll, he paid me no heed. I viewed the ground ahead and saw that he stood on a single large rock—one that I could dislodge while staying outside the sphere of his defense.

"And so I sheathed my sword, found the edge of the rock, gripped it with my fingers, and pulled upward with all my strength. At first, the rock did not budge. But I was determined to repay the favor I owed the stableboy, and so I gathered every ounce of my might and pulled harder. At last, the rock did rip from the earth and upend the troll. Both my opponent and his weapon fell to the rocky ground. Quickly I dashed toward the club and clasped it in my right hand. I could feel the power of the weapon as I gripped it, and I leapt into the air to strike the troll. I rendered the troll insensate with but a single blow, leaving the path free to the Eye of Gerda."

"Did you keep the club?"

Sif chuckled. "I did bring the club back with me to Asgard, along with the jewel. 'Twas Frigga who identified the club as the mighty Sigivald, and I did turn it over to her."

That confused Hilde. "Why didn't you keep it?"

"The sword is my preferred weapon." Sif shrugged. "Clubs are for trolls."

Hilde shook her head. "But if it guarantees victory . . ."

"As Frigga did explain—and as I proved—the enchantment grants whoever *wields* the club victory. The moment one stops wielding it, victory is no longer assured. Besides, with magic, the simpler the spell seems, the more complicated it truly is . . . and it is never reliable, not even in the trustworthy hands of someone noble like Frigga—never mind a foul creature like Loki, or Amora, the Enchantress, or Karnilla, the Norn Queen."

"I guess."

"In any event, even as I gave Sigivald to Frigga, I did provide the stableboy with his gift for his bride-to-be. It was only when he presented it to her and her face fell in shock that the truth did come out."

"So did they get married?" Hilde asked eagerly.

Sif shook her head. "As soon as the boy realized that she had tricked him—and, by extension, me—he refused to marry her."

"That's really awful. She should have just *said*."

"Indeed." Sif got to her feet. "'Tis always better to speak one's mind than keep one's peace, particularly about matters of the heart. When I was your age, I wished to be taught the ways of the sword as Thor, Fandral, and the other boys were. So I went and asked for ingress into the lessons. As a girl, I was not offered such a place, so I spoke my mind."

With a grin, Hilde said, "And when I wanted to come up this mountain with you, I asked!"

"Which," Sif said admonishingly, "is a preferable gambit than simply sneaking along the Gopul River and hoping I would not notice until it was too late."

Hilde looked down. "I know." Then she looked up and smiled. "That's *why* I asked this morning."

"Good girl." Sif hauled her pack up. "Let us continue."

They spent most of the afternoon working their way up the mountain before making camp. Hilde slept peacefully through the night. Sif, for her part, slept very little. She could not ask Hilde to take a watch, and she did not wish them to both be asleep at the same time. Sif did allow herself a quick nap toward sunrise, but that was all.

As they proceeded upward, Hilde climbed up a set of rocks and cried out, "Sif! I found something!"

Sif, who had been behind the girl, climbed faster to catch up.

Hilde had made it up to a plateau, and as soon as Sif

joined her, the girl pointed at the rocks on the ground. "Look at this!"

As her teacher, Sif wanted to make sure that the child truly saw what she should have been seeing. "At what am I looking, Hilde?"

"Can't you see it? It's obvious!" Letting out a huff, Hilde pointed at another set of rocks behind her. "See, over there, the rock patterns are just like they are everywhere else." Then she pointed back at the first set of rocks. "But these are all messed up—like someone's been up here disturbing them."

Sif nodded. She too had noticed that, but she was glad that Hilde had also done so.

Hilde then said, "I think I'd better go back to Flodbjerge."

At that, Sif blinked. She had, in fact, been trying to figure out how to break it to Hilde that once they were able to determine the dragon's general location, Volstagg's daughter should return to the village. She had not expected the child to suggest it on her own.

Holding up her hands, Hilde said, "I know what you're going to say, but I can make it back okay on my own. And I already saw the dragon twice—I think that's enough."

Sif chuckled. "You are wise beyond your years, young Hilde. Go forth and return to the village. Upon your arrival, do look in upon Regin, to be sure that he is safe in the storehouse."

Hilde nodded. "I will. Good luck against the dragon!"

With that, Hilde started her long climb down the mountain.

* * *

Volstagg's daughter was glad she was able to put Sif's lessons to good use, but the story Sif had told the day before was what really stuck with her.

The truth was that Hilde was frightened of the dragon. And she *hated* that. She wanted to be like Sif, who wasn't afraid of anything.

But she thought about what Sif had said about forcing her way into a sword-fighting lesson when she had been Hilde's age. Sif had known what she wanted, and she went after it.

Hilde wanted to be like that.

However, the more she thought about it, the more she realized that she'd seen quite enough of Oter. The dragon was big and mean and scary, and Sif had barely managed to survive their last encounter. Yes, Hilde wanted to be like Sif, but she also knew that she wasn't like Sif yet, and wouldn't be for some time. Being able to track a doe and find traces of a dragon's path were a long way from becoming as great a warrior as Sif.

Hilde would get there eventually. Until then, she was

content to remain as far away from the big, scary dragon as possible.

Going down the mountain was far faster than going up, and besides, Hilde could move faster when she wasn't slowed down by Sif. For someone so big, she sure moved slowly!

As a result, their day-and-a-half journey up the mountain was less than a day's journey down, and the sun was only starting to set by the time Hilde reached the village.

She went to the council hall to report in to Helena and the others, but she only saw Bjorn.

"Hilde!" he cried upon seeing her enter the hall. "What news? Where is Sif?"

Quickly, Hilde filled in Bjorn on what had transpired.

Nodding sagely, Bjorn said, "You were wise to return. In truth, I had thought it odd that Sif would allow you to go along."

Hilde grinned. "My father says I'm very good at getting my way."

Taking her leave, Hilde set off in the direction of the storehouse. The large building was far away from anything else, and with her newfound awareness of tracking, she saw that there were very few footprints on the ground.

In fact, she saw only two sets—one going toward the storehouse, and one going away from it.

She recalled that the storehouse had gotten very little use of late—which was why Oter hadn't attacked it, and why Sif had thought it a good location for the dragon's brother to hide in.

A wave of cold overcame her as she drew closer to the structure. The spell that kept the fish chilled and preserved until winter was obviously very effective. The handle to the storehouse door was ice cold to the touch, and Hilde had to pull her hand away and blow on it to warm it up before touching the handle again.

Touching the handle more gingerly, she pushed it down. The door clicked open.

"Hello? Regin, it's Hilde—are you here?"

The storehouse was not lit, so sunlight alone illuminated the frost-covered boxes stacked inside.

"Regin?"

Leaving the door open so she could see, Hilde moved between the boxes.

"Regin?"

Eventually, she found a pallet and a blanket—but no sign of Regin.

Frowning, Hilde ran back to the door. She checked the footprints again.

Both sets had been left by the same feet. Based on the amount of wear on the edges of the tracks, the ones coming to the storehouse were almost two days old.

But the ones moving away from it were about half a day

old. If they were Regin's prints, he had left in the middle of the night—probably so no one could see him.

Hilde followed the footprints away from the storehouse. Sif had instructed Regin to stay in the storehouse—if he had sneaked out in the middle of the night, Hilde was honor bound to find out where he had gone.

CHAPTER NINE

Sif continued her search for the dragon's lair in the many caves that dotted this section of the Valhalla Mountains.

The signs of the dragon's passing were extensive. The plateaus hereabouts were not wide, and the dragon was of sufficient girth to make navigating on his four legs without causing significant damage to the surrounding terrain difficult. Not that Oter had any great need for stealth or subtlety. As a dragon, such traits were of little use—even less so in such a remote a hiding place.

Sif was able to immediately dismiss several caves as too small for Oter to fit comfortably inside. She inspected each of the larger caves, and knew upon approaching the third such cave that it was the location of Oter's hoard. Afternoon sunlight reflected off the gold that was only a short distance from the cave mouth, glinting in Sif's eye.

Of Oter himself, she found no sign.

The cave was not terribly deep, but was quite wide. The gold and jewels were strewn about the space, taking up the entirety of the cave's floor, but spread out and flattened by the dragon's heavy form taking its rest upon the hoard.

Sif also saw several bones littering the outer edges of the

cave. They were large enough to be those of bears and other creatures that roamed these mountains, and which had no doubt provided food for the dragon. One set of bones was fresh, with bloodstains still upon them. Oter had, it seemed, fed recently.

Those were not the only bloodstains, however—the cave was spotted with the creature's own ichor, no doubt borne from Sif's sword wound.

Moving back to the cave mouth, she closed her eyes and listened. In addition to the sound of the wind and the occasional chirp of nearby birds, Sif also heard the low rumble of water cascading down the mountain.

Since the dragon had just fed, perhaps he now was drinking from the nearby stream.

Unsheathing Gunnvarr, she ran in the direction of the water.

Coming over a ridge, she saw both a stream and the dragon lapping up water from it, her own sword still jutting from his back. The dragon stood near a hollowed-out tree that had been uprooted, and which lay beside the water's edge.

Unfortunately, Sif had been so focused on getting to the dragon that she had neglected her own lessons to Hilde and the other children with regard to sneaking up on one's prey. She had lumbered through the plateau with no more regard for stealth than Oter himself had shown.

The dragon looked up with his horned head as Sif cleared the ridge.

"You again! I had hoped to have another opportunity to rend you limb from limb, little girl! How considerate of you to come to me, rather than forcing me to search the entire town to locate you again."

"Your reign of terror ends today, Oter."

"I have no 'reign of terror,' little girl. I merely wish to ensure that I retain what is rightfully mine!"

"Cursed gold stolen from the dwarves rightfully belongs to no one save the dwarves," Sif said. "And the people of Flodbjerge are indeed terrorized. Call it what you will, but the villagers live in fear of you—and that fear will end today!"

Sif leapt from the ridge to the dragon's head even as Oter's flame singed the bottom of her boots. She took hold of one of the creature's horns as she arced through the air.

Screaming, Oter threw his neck back and forth, but Sif maintained her grip.

To her surprise, the horn itself gave way before her grip did. It broke off with a snap that echoed off the mountain, sending Sif and the creature's now-severed appendage falling to the water below.

Sif landed in the shallow stream with a bone-bruising thud, Gunnvarr in her right hand and the dragon's jagged-edged horn in her left.

Oter's screams echoed through the Valhalla Mountains, to the point that Sif feared the choosers of the slain themselves could hear.

The dragon craned his neck downward and screamed again—his scream this time accompanied by fire.

Quickly, Sif rolled to her right, narrowly avoiding the flames that issued forth from the dragon's maw that boiled away the section of stream in which she'd been lying.

She clambered to her feet, stared at the horn for a moment, then ran back toward the ridge.

She had to remove the dragon from his hoard, and it would do little good to fight him here at the stream. He needed to be defeated in the cave.

Sif jumped onto the hollowed-out tree and leapt over the ridge, narrowly avoiding another gout of flame. Sheathing Gunnvarr and taking the horn in her right hand, she stood upright and hurled it at Oter's head.

The horn ripped into Oter's nostril, causing the creature to once again scream to the heavens.

Sif ran back toward the cave as Oter cried out, "You will pay for this, little girl! My vengeance will be terrible and merciless!"

While Sif's booted feet carried her across the plateau to the cave quickly, the dragon's wings were speedier, and Oter landed at the cave mouth ahead of her. Without breaking stride, Sif dodged to her right as the dragon again tried to burn her.

She rolled and came up to her feet, running toward the dragon's left side. The terrain worked in her favor, as Oter could not maneuver as easily as she could on the narrow plateau, and Sif easily was able to slide Gunnvarr between two scales on his side. She yanked out the blade just as quickly, not wishing to lose another weapon to the creature's hide.

Oter tried to use his tail to strike Sif, but she rolled under that blow as well, coming upright underneath the dragon's belly. Again she thrust Gunnvarr upward, and again the blade sliced into Oter's scaly hide. The creature screamed in agony, and Sif took advantage of his pain to scramble out from under him.

She leapt onto Oter's back, crawling over to where her own sword still jutted out.

Gripping the hilt with her free hand, she yanked with all her might. The sword came free, loosing quite a bit of Oter's lifeblood with it.

And then Sif leapt up again, to another portion of the dragon's expansive back, and slashed twice, once with each sword.

Imitating the flight of a mosquito, Sif jumped about the dragon's form, slashing each spot with one blade, the other, or both.

With each fresh cut, Sif felt the exhilaration of battle. From the time she was a little girl, she'd dreamt of it, and she still recalled her first true test. She'd sparred plenty of times as part of Tyr's lessons, but that kind of combat had no real stakes.

No, her first real test had come when she had answered Odin's call to arms in Vanaheim, even though she had not been one of the ones Odin had called. But she had gone into battle to face the trolls who attacked the Vanir. In particular, she remembered facing one such troll who had attempted to strike her, but the massive size of his arms made his punches easy to see coming, and Sif's smaller, lithe form had dodged the blows easily. Her own strength had not yet reached its full peak—she was still a girl, not yet the mighty woman she would grow into—but it was still greater than most, and she had been able to triumph against the larger foe.

In that moment, when she had defeated her first enemy in combat, Sif had felt more alive than ever before during her then-brief years. Everything else had fallen to the side— Tyr's disdain, Thor's friendship (more than friendship, actually, though it would be many years before she would realize it), Odin's power, Heimdall's love, and the confusion of the other children of Asgard, who did not understand why a girl wished to join the men on the field of battle.

All of that had burnt away, replaced only by the impera- tive of stopping those who would menace Vanaheim. She wasn't a girl, she wasn't a woman, she wasn't Heimdall's sister, she wasn't a citizen of Asgard. She was only a warrior, and nothing else mattered but the glory of noble combat. When she, Thor, Fandral, and the other warriors had returned to Asgard triumphant, Heimdall had said to her, "I've always known, sister, that you were as mighty as the men of Asgard, and today you proved it."

Though Heimdall had never said as much in the past, Sif knew that her brother's gift was to see what others did not, and so he had always known that she had the heart of a warrior born.

On that day, she became determined to show it to everyone else, as well.

And so she sought out more battles. And every time she went into combat—whether against trolls, dwarves, elves, giants, demons, orcs, aliens, vampires, her fellow gods, or one of Midgard's many supervillains—she tried to recapture that exhilaration.

"Enough!" The dragon's cries returned Sif to the here and now.

Oter spread his wings and took to the air in the hope of shaking off his foe.

Sif lost her balance, but managed to use the dragon's scales as handholds to keep herself from falling to the ground.

And then she smiled. Why was she trying to stay on the creature's back when it was no longer a sound tactic?

She dove off the dragon, plummeting to the ground. She landed surely on her feet, her might causing the rock to crumble and buckle beneath her boots. Climbing out of the two divots she'd created, she looked up to see Oter circling the cave from above.

"You are a fool, little girl. You would have been safer on my back."

"If I am the fool, Oter," Sif yelled, "why is it that you have left your hoard where I might easily take it?"

Oter's face constricted into a rictus of anguish. "No!"

Grinning, Sif sheathed Gunnvarr and ran toward the dragon's cave, her own sword still gripped in her left hand.

"You will not have my hoard, little girl! No one shall! It's mine, I tell you, *mine*!"

Sif ran into the cave and climbed atop the pile of gold.

Oter landed and shoved his head into the cave mouth. "You will never steal what is mine, little girl—never!"

As the dragon breathed fire into the cave, Sif dove into the pile of gold.

While the many coins and jewels did protect Sif from being burnt, the precious metals also conducted heat. Rapidly, Sif found herself baking in her ruby-colored armor.

But still she waited, braving the agonizing heat, until she no longer heard her foe's exhalation.

As soon as the sound of the flame stopped reverberating in her ears, she cried out in pain and pushed herself out of the pile of gold. Once she gained her footing, she whipped her sword around in the air, hoping to catch Oter off guard, but her vision was blurred from the great heat of the enflamed hoard. Indeed, the cave itself was oppressively hot from the dragon's flames, little better than being amidst the heated gold.

Taking advantage of Sif's failed swing, Oter did something she never expected. Just as her vision cleared, Sif saw the dragon open his giant maw, and she braced herself for the onslaught of flame.

Instead, Oter leaned in and engulfed Sif in his mouth. His jaws snapped shut, the force of his teeth yanking Sif from her feet.

Darkness consumed Sif. As hot and oppressive as the cave had become, it was as nothing compared to the inferno that was the dragon's mouth.

Sif felt the pull of the dragon's throat as the creature attempted to swallow her whole. She thrust her sword downward, piercing the dragon's serpentine tongue.

Light flooded the creature's maw as Oter opened his mouth to scream in agony. Sif yanked out the sword, hoping to take advantage of his cries to escape, but the dragon closed his mouth too quickly.

But her action had resulted in one beneficial consequence—Oter was no longer trying to swallow. Sif reared back with her right hand and punched through the dragon's teeth, her mighty blow shattering his incisors.

Somersaulting through the newly created hole, Sif rolled onto the ground and brought herself upright.

Oter had removed his head from the cavern and was thrashing about the plateau, the many injuries Sif had inflicted adding up significantly. His tail flew back and forth wildly, and Sif was unable to dodge it. The scaly appendage slammed into her side, and Sif went hurtling out of the cave, across the plateau, and down the mountain.

At first, Sif had no control of her actions, and flailed wildly as she tumbled down the mountain. But after several seconds, she was able to grab on to one of the outcropped rocks and halt her descent—though the suddenness of that stop nearly ripped her arm from its socket.

For a moment, Sif simply hung from the rock by her right hand, regaining her composure. She had lost her grip on her sword, and it continued to tumble down the mountain, no doubt lost forever. Luckily, the scabbard Bjorn had provided remained strapped to her back, with Gunnvarr sheathed inside.

Sif reached up and grabbed another stone with her left hand, securing herself on the rock face. She paused for a moment, caught her breath, and then hauled herself upward. Perched atop the rock, she looked up and saw no sign of Oter.

Confused, she continued to climb, remaining vigilant. But the dragon was nowhere to be seen—not in the sky, nor on the plateau. She did not hear him gloating or breathing fire.

Sif redoubled her efforts, climbing faster. Shortly, she reached the passageway she and Hilde had taken up the mountain, and which led to the outcropping where Hilde had discovered the dragon's tracks. At the top, she unsheathed Gunnvarr and ran to the cave.

She feared that Oter had decided to take advantage of her absence to renew his search in Flodbjerge for Regin.

That fear, at least, was allayed by the sounds she heard closer to the cave—Oter was talking inside it. The stone walls muffled his exact words, but it was definitely the drag-on's rumbling voice she heard.

Sif slowed as she drew near, sword at the ready, taking care to move with greater stealth. If the dragon was dis-tracted by something in the cave, she would use it to her advantage.

A few steps from the entrance, she began to be able to make out the dragon's words. His voice was different, the consonants slurred, no doubt due to Sif's violent removal of several of his teeth.

". . . will never depart from you for long. You will always remain under my watchful eye. Nothing shall take you from me, not the foul goddess of Asgard, not my idiot brother, not our pathetic father, not that incompetent bandit, and not the dwarf who turned me into this awful creature when

I took possession of you. Soon, we will need to move to a new cave, for this one grows too unstable, but worry not—you will stay mine forever."

Shaking her head, Sif moved quietly into the cave. She inched toward Oter's tail, which moved slowly back and forth near the mouth of the cave.

Sif debated the efficacy of her thinking. Had she retained both swords, her plan would have been a far better one.

Gazing upon the dragon's form, she saw that many of the cuts she had inflicted were already mostly healed. Even her swords, forged as they were from Asgardian metal, did not penetrate far into Oter's hide.

No, the sword was not the best weapon to use against the dragon. And she had proven with her escape from Oter's mouth that her strength was perhaps a greater ally than her steel, particularly given the goal of saving Oter rather than killing him, as Regin had requested.

So Sif raised Gunnvarr over her head and brought it down point-first on the end of Oter's tail, impaling the appendage fully.

The dragon bellowed, his tail pinned to the ground at the cave entrance, but the creature's continued cries only served to make Sif's warrior heart beat faster.

"Why won't you die, little girl?"

"I think, in truth, that I prefer 'foul goddess' to 'little girl.'"

"I will call you 'dead'!" Oter turned his neck and breathed

fire. Sif dove to the side of the entrance and easily dodged the flames as they shot through the cave mouth.

Awkwardly, the dragon attempted to remove himself from the cavern, but he was hampered by his pinned tail. He twisted and turned and screamed and contorted—all to no avail.

Then came Sif's fists, for the warrior woman did not stand idle while the creature thrashed about.

"No longer shall you torment the people of Flodbjerge, nor shall you threaten my own life!"

She struck a huge blow to the dragon's jaw, then another to the side of his head.

"For I am Sif, and ever have I been the victor over any foe foolish enough to cross my path!"

Again she struck the dragon, punching downward on his snout and causing his head to bounce off the floor next to his tail.

"And you will not be the winner this day—nor any day after this!"

She kicked the dragon in the jaw, sending his head flying upward, flipping the contorted creature around until he landed on his back atop his hoard.

Jumping atop the dragon's chest, Sif continued to pummel him, punching him again and again, until Oter no longer moved.

Breathing heavily, Sif wiped her brow and climbed down off the dragon's body.

Slowly, Sif stumbled toward Oter's tail. Wearily clasping Gunnvarr's hilt, she yanked it upward. But fatigue sapped her strength, and it took several tries to free the sword.

Eventually, though, she did loose it. After wiping the ichor and dirt off the blade and onto Oter's scales, she sheathed Gunnvarr and wrapped both hands firmly around the end of the dragon's tail.

Regin had said that Oter had to be defeated and removed from his hoard. She had accomplished the first. Now, it was time to do the second.

Gathering every ounce of her waning strength, Sif pulled until her arms felt as if they would fly from her shoulders. She pulled until sweat obscured her vision. She pulled until every sinew of her body cried out with sharp, brutal pain.

She pulled until she felt she could not pull anymore, and then she pulled harder.

Inch by inch, the dragon's heavy serpentine body slid across the piles of gold and jewels, across the rocky ground, and out onto the plateau.

Her strength all but spent, Sif leaned back as far as she could and yanked the dragon's head out of the cave.

As soon as Oter was no longer touching any of his treasured hoard, the dragon did start to glow.

Gasping, Sif stepped backward.

She watched as Oter's snout started to shrink and his wings began to recede. The four short legs disappeared, while the tail split in two. His watery yellow eyes shrank and became blue, while his remaining horn reformed itself into a mop of blond hair.

Within moments, the transformation was complete. Tail had become legs, wings had become arms, and the dragon's face had become a human visage.

Oter was human once again. The curse had been broken.

And not a moment too soon, for her exertions had taken their toll, and Sif's knees buckled beneath her. She collapsed to the ground, in desperate need of rest.

In a haze, she thought she heard someone coming up behind her.

Had Hilde returned? Who else would be on this mountain?

"Well done, milady," said a familiar voice before something heavy collided with her head and the world went dark.

CHAPTER TEN

Sif was only insensate for a few minutes, but by the time her head cleared, her hands had been bound behind her and she had been seated with her back against the cave wall.

Next to her, Oter was still unconscious, lying naked on the cave's stone floor, also bound.

Standing over her was Regin, with a vicious smile on his face. He now wore Bjorn's scabbard—Gunnvarr sheathed within—leaving Sif unarmed.

"R-Regin? What—"

"I apologize, milady, for the mistreatment—especially given the great favor you have done me. But you might endeavor to impede my actions, and I cannot have that."

Sif's mind remained fogged from exhaustion and the blow she had suffered. She shook her head, trying to clear her mind.

"I must also apologize for the story I spun before you and the council." Regin smiled ruefully. "I did mislead you a bit, but it was necessary."

While he spoke, Sif pushed against her bonds, but Regin had done his knot-work well. She could barely budge her wrists.

Her head still felt as if it were filled with cotton, but she needed to figure out a way to get out of these bonds. She needed to keep Regin talking. "You did not entirely mislead me. The method by which Oter could be reverted to his natural state was exactly as you described."

"Well, of course, because that was the goal. But in furtherance of that goal, I did prevaricate somewhat with regard to my relationship with my father—and my brother."

"What do you mean?"

Regin smiled. "When I told you of how I grew up, I suppose I gave you the impression that my brother and I were happy with Hreidmar, our father." He looked away. "It must be so nice for you Asgardians. Your lives are so pure and simple. Someone attacks Asgard, and you defend it. Odin tells you what to do, and you do it. No one ever defies him, because he's Odin."

"If you believe that, then you are a fool. The All-Father is mighty and wise, but he is not perfect. I myself have defied Odin—alongside Thor, the Warriors Three, and Balder— and we were exiled to Midgard in punishment. Many times have Thor and Loki defied Odin, and he is their father as well as their king." She chuckled. "And if you believe my life is pure and simple, then you know nothing of my life."

"Perhaps. But Odin's punishments for defiance from his offspring are *nothing*—I know this, because the Trickster and the thunder god both still live! My mother, however, was not so fortunate. Tell me, milady, when you were a small girl, did you wake up every morning wondering if this was the day that you would die by the angry hand of your father? Did you and Heimdall cower together in fear every night before going to sleep? If not—and it is obvious that is *not* the case—then I believe I may remain secure in my pronouncement of pure and simple for your life amongst the Aesir."

Sif felt a pang of sympathy, but she tamped it down. This man had attacked her in secret and bound her—he had made himself her enemy, and Sif refused to sympathize with her enemies.

Regin continued. "Our mother defied Hreidmar just as you claim Thor and Loki have defied Odin. But where Thor's worst punishment was—what did you say? Exile to Midgard?—my mother would have longed for something as painless as *exile*. No, she paid for her defiance with her life. And Hreidmar made it abundantly clear that we would suffer the same fate if we were to say anything." He snorted. "Not that it mattered. We lived in Nastrond under King Fafnir, where the only law was not to anger Fafnir. Had we told anyone of Mother's death, there would have been no consequences anyway."

"Nastrond was a foul place indeed. Odin had good reason for destroying it," Sif said quietly.

Regin smiled viciously. "You speak intemperately, milady."

"I speak the truth. You told us that your mother died giving birth to your stillborn brother."

"Mother almost did die that day. The labor was difficult, and the fetus was long dead when she finally birthed it. Hreidmar was furious, as he wanted another child, and so beat Mother severely. But *that* day she survived. No, it was when she attempted to run away that Hreidmar did finish the task of her murder."

"Were you even attacked by Siegfried the bandit, then?"

"Not attacked, no." Regin shook his head. "After Mother's death, the story continues much as I told it, with one notable exception. The pelt business was lucrative for our father, but not for the pair of us—and not for Hreidmar for very long, either. Whatever profits we made were quickly poured down our father's gullet. At first, he would drink at home, but then he started to go to a local tavern—alone. That was the first time we attempted to run away. But he caught us, and took us with him to the tavern from that day forward."

Sif shook her head. "You are hardly the first children to be all but raised in a tavern."

"Oh, Hreidmar did us a favor by bringing us there. It was how we met Siegfried. You see, we did not encounter the bandit for the first time on the road to Gundersheim, but rather one night at the tavern. Siegfried saw how Hreidmar treated us, and he saw that we feared to confront him ourselves. He suggested that we pay someone to kill him. We agreed, but we were stymied by a lack of coin with which to make the payment. It was Siegfried who told us of a dwarf passing through Nastrond with a hoard of gold that he intended to use to pay for a large patch of land upon which he wished to build a smithy.

"You were correct, milady, when you mentioned that a proper bandit should never attack alone, which was why Siegfried did not wish to attempt to steal the gold alone. In fact, he did not wish to steal it himself at all—for while Siegfried was strong, he was also lame. He did not trust that he would be able to move quickly enough to make an escape following an act of banditry. We were both in need—he of someone to provide whole legs for the act, and we of someone who could rid us of our father.

"So we came to an agreement. The treasure stolen from the dwarf would be split three ways. Siegfried did distract Hreidmar at the tavern while Oter and I stole the gold from the dwarf."

"I take it that you and Oter reneged on the arrangement?"

Regin nodded. "Hreidmar had taught us that loyalty was something to be bought and sold, or received through intimidation. Of what use was it to us? Siegfried offered to kill our father, and what reason did we have for recompense once it was done?"

"But you still killed him?" Sif asked. She had been straining against her bonds, and they were starting to give way.

All she needed to do was keep Regin talking while she freed herself.

"Eventually, yes, we did kill Siegfried. The death of our father occurred in much the same way as I described it to you in Flodbjerge, with Siegfried 'ambushing' us on the road to Gundersheim, where we were taking our wares to market. Siegfried acted as a bandit out to steal from us—and as we had predicted, Hreidmar did attack him violently. Siegfried was able to kill Hreidmar with ease—and then he demanded his share of the treasure. Of course, we had it not with us, as we had needed to keep it hidden from our father. We told Siegfried to meet us at a cabin in the Norn Forest." Regin laughed. "I must confess, milady, that I could not tell you if such a cabin does exist in that forest. It was a creation of my brother and I, merely a place to send Siegfried on a fool's errand."

"You said you killed him, not sent him on a fool's errand."

"That, milady, is because *we* were the fools." Regin started to pace the mouth of the cave. "Siegfried doubled back and followed us to where we had stored the gold. But as soon as Oter entered the chamber where the gold was housed, he started to change. You see, he had been the one to steal the gold. My role had been to guard the dwarf and keep him from interfering. For this reason, the curse was Oter's alone to bear."

Sif shook her head, even as one thumb came free of her bonds. "So there was no charm that left you immune?"

Regin snorted. "I doubt any such charm even exists, but I required it to add verisimilitude to my story."

"Well done," Sif said dryly. Her index finger was now loose, as well. It was only a matter of time. If she could just get her middle finger free, she'd be able to grip the ropes and snap them in two.

"In any event, Oter transformed into a dragon. I was able to escape his wrath, but Siegfried was not so fortunate. The day after I made my escape, I returned to find the place empty of all save a dwarf. That part of my tale was the truth—the dwarf had come in search of his gold, but found only me. He spared me because I had *not* transformed into a dragon, and therefore he believed me to be innocent of the theft."

"So it was not a coincidence," Sif said, "that you came to Flodbjerge to live."

"For *years* I have searched for my brother so I could claim the treasure! My initial belief was that I should have half of it, but I have seen how the people of the village below live in terror of the dragon. *That* is even greater than the wealth that the dwarf's treasure would bring me. I want the *power* that comes with the dragon form. So now, I will claim the entire hoard and become the figure of fear that my brother was!"

Sif continued to struggle to get a second finger free. Whatever else one could say about Hreidmar, he had obviously taught at least one of his sons ropecraft, as Regin's knot was tight indeed.

She needed to stall him further, and so she asked, "And what will being such a figure grant you? The fates of many of the dragons of the Nine Worlds have already been written, and they bode ill for you. Will you become like Nidhogg, condemned to chew on a root of Yggdrasil forevermore, waiting at the gates to Hela's realm? Will you become as the Midgard Serpent, trapped beneath the earth of that world? Will you become like your former monarch, Fafnir, transformed into a dragon and slain in battle with Thor? Stories about dragons invariably have ill endings for those creatures."

"I do not have the ambitions of those creatures, milady. I will be content to have the fools of Flodbjerge look upon me with fear."

"Your ambitions are of no interest to me, Regin. Be assured that if you take this track, you simply will become another dragon that I have bested."

Regin snorted. "Just because you defeated my brother—"

"I speak not of your brother, but of the mighty Lindworm of Denmark on Midgard."

"And you defeated him?"

"I killed the creature before he could wreak any more havoc on Midgard, yes. I had come to Midgard in search of a baby dragon that had escaped from Asgard. I found that it had been given as a wedding gift to Queen Thora when she married King Ragnar Lothbrok. They thought it a harmless pet, but it quickly grew to an immense size and started to consume the livestock of the land.

"King Ragnar had sent many of his soldiers to do battle against the creature, which he had dubbed the Lindworm of Denmark, but those few who returned alive did so without having succeeded. The king's subjects were in danger of starving, for the animals they used to plow the fields and as food were being taken by the dragon.

"You would have liked King Ragnar, Regin, because he, too, dismissed me when I approached him. I told him that I was of the Aesir, and while Queen Thora and most of his subjects knelt before me, King Ragnar only scoffed.

"'You are Thor's bedmate, little girl,' he said to me. 'Of what use are you to me against the Lindworm?'

"I set my jaw as I stared at him and said, 'Thor is sometimes privileged to share my bed, yes, but that is often after we have shared a battle together. I have defeated every foe I have ever faced, as evidenced by the fact that I still live and they do not.'

"King Ragnar stood and cried, 'The men I sent to battle the Lindworm all could make similar boasts before facing the creature. You are just a girl, what could you *possibly* do that they could not?'

"I smiled and said, 'Win.'

"Throwing up his hands, Ragnar said, 'You are a goddess, and I am but a king. Who am I to stop you from going to your doom?'

"What I did not know at the time was that King Ragnar had promised the hand of his daughter, Aslaug, to the warrior who defeated the Lindworm, and he feared my victory, as it would force him to go back on his word, which would damage his reputation amongst his people.

"But nonetheless I struck out into the fields and tracked down the Lindworm. It was not difficult to find him, for he was even larger than your brother was when in his reptilian form, as he had consistently been dining on oxen, cows, bulls, and horses.

"I raised my sword and attacked the creature. The battle lasted many hours, and the Lindworm did wound me grievously, but its underbelly was its weak point, and I was able to strike it there with my sword.

"After killing the Lindworm, I sliced its head from its body and brought it to King Ragnar. Only then did I learn of his promise regarding Aslaug—and so I claimed her as was my right. She was a clever, talented child, skilled in playing the harp. I took her with me across the rainbow bridge back to Asgard and fed her the Golden Apples of Immortality, and to this day she remains one of the musicians who plays for Odin at the palace."

As Sif finished the tale of her battle against the Lindworm, she at last managed to get a second finger free.

Regin gave a small bow. "You are to be commended, milady, for that victory, and for all your others—particularly the one against my brother. But while you may have presented the All-Father with a harpist when you defeated the Lindworm, the only gift Odin will receive this day is your cooling corpse."

Regin walked toward the cave as Sif tugged on her bonds, at last having the maneuverability to add to her strength to the effort.

By the time she snapped the ropes and got to her feet, Regin was inside Oter's cave. Following him in, Sif watched in horror as the very transformation she had observed with Oter a short time ago happened again—only in reverse. Regin's face lengthened, his form grew, his arms flattened and expanded, his legs fused together, and his skin turned a scaly black.

Now fully transformed, Regin looked down upon Sif with eyes as yellow and as watery as his brother's had been, though the surrounding scales were of a darker hue. His voice rang out with the same rumbling tone as his brother's, but the words were sharper and even more brutal.

"I am grateful to you, Lady Sif. You have done what I could not, which is defeat my brother and remove the curse. In gratitude, I promise you the mercy of a quick death."

With that, Regin reared back his head and prepared to breathe his newfound fire at Sif.

CHAPTER ELEVEN

Propelling herself upward with her legs, Sif did a backflip that kept her from being broiled by Regin's fiery breath. Regin turned his head upward in the hope of catching Sif in midair, but her flip was far faster than Regin could crane his unfamiliar neck.

Sitting atop the hoard of wealth, Regin continued to try to burn his prey, but Sif was able to stay ahead of his exhalations. He had yet to master them as Oter had.

"Pathetic, Regin." That was Oter's voice.

Sif looked down and saw that Oter was now awake and struggling to sit upright. His speech was no longer the rumbling utterances of a dragon's mouth, but instead the tenor tones of a human one, tinged with a lisp because of his missing front teeth, an injury that had remained through the transformation.

Regin emitted a chuckle that sounded like two rocks grinding together. "So, brother, you are awake. Good. I was hoping you would be able to look me in the eye when I finally rid the world of you."

"I was referring to your idiocy, Regin. You see, the cave in which *my* treasure resides is one I was going to abandon soon because the entrance is unstable. And you just breathed fire on it."

"What are you—"

Regin's words were interrupted by a sharp snapping sound as the rock that made up part of the cave mouth started to crack.

Sif ran over to the bound Oter, threw him over her shoulder, and escaped to the plateau.

Angry, Regin reared his head upward and again breathed fire, but for naught.

Seconds later, the entire cave mouth collapsed, burying Regin within. Outside, Sif tore away Oter's bonds.

"Thank you," he said, "but that won't hold him long. He is not as strong as I was, at least not yet, but he will be able to break free eventually."

"Do not think," Sif said angrily, "that I free you out of any consideration for your plight. I simply do not wish to carry you down the mountain."

"I understand. But *you* must understand that I was compelled to guard the hoard at all costs."

"And for that, you terrorized the people of Flodbjerge?"

Oter shook his head. "I have no enmity for the people of that village, milady."

"Oh, *now* I am 'milady'? It was not long ago, Oter, that I was 'little girl' or 'foul goddess.'"

Oter winced. "Yes, milady, I am sorry. As I said, I was compelled—you threatened my hoard."

"In truth, I threatened no such thing. I care not for gold or jewels or finery. My only interest was in saving the people of Flodbjerge."

Shaking his head, Oter let out a long sigh. "I had no quarrel with those good people, milady, believe me. I have lived in these mountains for some time. I did observe the people of the village covertly, but only to ensure that they posed no threat to my hoard. That state of affairs remained until—"

Sif nodded. "Until your brother came to live there."

"The dwarf's curse is vicious, milady. It amplified my belief that anyone might steal the treasure, but it also knew who I believed to pose the greatest threat to it. Of all those still living, only two people would trigger so intense a response of fear—the dwarf from whom I stole the gold, and my brother, who desired it almost as much as I."

A rumble came from beneath the rocks from the cave-in. Sif knew that it was just a matter of moments before Regin broke loose. "Come," she said, leading Oter toward the ridge.

Oter spoke as they hurried. "The compulsion to find my brother overwhelmed all else. I only was kept from searching the village all at once because I could not bear to be far from my treasure for very long."

"I assumed as much," Sif said with a nod.

The rocks that covered the cave mouth were now shaking

faster. Oter glanced back apprehensively, and then regarded Sif with urgency. "He will be free in a moment. You have one advantage against my brother that you did not have against me. After so many years, my hide grew thick and nigh-impenetrable. But Regin's scales are weaker, thinner— you may easily penetrate his flesh with your blade, as you could not mine."

Sif blew out a breath through clenched teeth. "That presents a certain difficulty, I'm afraid. I have no blade at the moment."

"What do you mean? You attacked me with *two* swords!"

She indicated the cave and its about-to-be-reopened entrance with her head. "Your brother took one of my swords when he rendered me unconscious. It is buried along with your erstwhile treasure. And my other sword fell down the mountain."

"That is a bit of an issue," Oter muttered.

"You understate greatly," Sif said dryly. "Nonetheless, Regin both lied to me and used me—neither of these offenses I am like to forgive. And his punishment for the same will be extremely severe."

As if on cue, Regin broke through the cave-in, sending stones flying in all directions. Sif moved to protect Oter from the debris. They were distant enough that the rocks bounced harmlessly off her armor, but Oter was completely unclothed and unprotected.

"You will pay for that indignity, Sif!" Regin cried out.

Sif whirled upon him. "Indignity? You lied to me, misled me, used me as your pawn—and worst of all, you caused the good people of Flodbjerge to suffer and die because of your very presence!"

Regin roared to the heavens, fire issuing forth from his snout. "How dare you take Oter's side after all he did!"

"I take only the side of the innocents who have suffered at the hands of *both* of you! I have no love for your miscreant of a brother—"

Oter whirled on her, taking offense at her words, but Sif ignored him and continued.

"—but at least he was compelled by a curse. You endangered the village while fully in what should laughingly be referred to as your right mind, and you did so for the most base of motives—greed!"

"Not greed, milady, *justice*! Oter did not suffer alone at the hands of our father—we were *both* the victims of his madness! The spoils of Hreidmar's and Siegfried's deaths should have been for *both* of us to share, and Oter took it away from me!"

Oter stepped forward. "You *imbecile*! You thrice-damned *fool*! This treasure would only be considered 'spoils' in the sense that it will spoil your life—as it *ruined* mine!"

Now Regin laughed heartily, more fire spewing forth. "*I'm* the imbecile? You had uncounted wealth—"

Oter interrupted his brother. "Of what use is wealth if it may not be spent? I desired to keep the dwarf's treasure so that we could have all the things that our father denied us. But the curse robbed me of that! Instead, I was trapped in this mountain range, able only to hoard the treasure—never to *use* it!"

"It matters not," Regin said. "The treasure is mine."

"No," Sif said, "the treasure is the dwarf's. And it will be returned to him once I dispose of you, as I did your brother."

"Hardly."

And with that, Regin flew into the air—and then careened past Sif and Oter.

Oter smiled. "It takes some time to accustom oneself to flying."

"So it would seem." Sif grabbed Oter and forcibly sat him next to the ridge. "Remain here. You will be safe."

"What will become of me?"

Sif looked up, trying to spy the dragon, but he had flown beyond her sight—at least temporarily. "If I defeat Regin, then both of you will be brought back to Asgard. Flodbjerge is under the All-Father's protection—it is why I came here in the first place—and Odin will decide both of your fates." She looked down at him. "If Regin defeats me, then I suspect that you will become his next victim in fairly short order. So pray that I win, for Odin will show you far more mercy than your brother will."

With that, Sif climbed atop the ridge, and saw Regin flying back toward her.

"You will die today, milady," Regin cried out as he hurtled through the air. "For millennia, they will sing songs of how Thor's paramour finally fell to Regin the dragon!"

Sif shook her head. "'Thor's paramour?' Is that all you see before you, Regin?"

"That is all you *are*, milady, as King Ragnar told you. Indeed, your story of the Lindworm is the first I have ever heard of such a battle. All the exploits of Sif that I had heard prior to this are solely in concert with a man of greater renown, whether it be Asgardian, mortal, or alien. The songs that they sing of Asgard are all of Thor's might and Balder's prowess and the camaraderie of the Warriors Three. If Sif is sung of at all, it is because of your exploits in the thunder god's bedchamber, not on the battlefield."

Laughing, Sif said, "You know the songs they sing of Asgard well, do you? I care little for them myself, as the measure of a warrior is not in songs that are sung. Warriors will ever be judged by how they fight, and how they win. And I have always fought, *little* dragon, and I have always won."

"Yes, riding through the countryside with a sword in your hand and a cry to arms in your heart. Yet now you have *no* sword. You face me unarmed and unprepared. Do you *truly* believe that there will be any outcome other than your death?"

"I have never believed otherwise. And I have always been right."

With that, Sif leapt into the air and landed atop the dragon's snout.

Regin thrashed about just as Oter had, but his thrashing proved far more dangerous, for his inexperience as a flyer meant chaos from his newfound wings. Both dragon and unwanted rider flew straight up, turned out into the open air, then back toward the mountain, crashing into its side with a jarring impact that rattled Sif in her armor.

Sif and Regin both tumbled down the mountain face, landing on the plateau.

Already fatigued from her battle with Oter the dragon and her struggle to remove his dead weight from the cave, and still smarting from the blow to her head inflicted by Regin, Sif now found her vision swimming before her as she tried to regain both her footing and her composure.

Clambering to her feet, Sif saw two dragons on the plateau. Closing her eyes tightly, she all but willed her vision to coalesce.

Opening her eyes again, she saw only one dragon—but one that was also getting to his taloned feet.

Crying out as she ran toward Regin, Sif jumped and punched the dragon directly in the snout. Another punch to the underside of his jaw sent the creature's head flying upward. He continued moving in that direction, again taking to the air.

Her offensive options limited by the dragon's flight, Sif went on the defensive, dodging Regin's renewed attempts to burn her alive. Regin's aim was far worse than Oter's had been, but Sif was moving much more slowly than usual.

In fact, one of Regin's exhalations did burn Sif's right arm, superheating her armor.

Her face twisting in fury and pain, Sif tore at her armor's right sleeve, ripping off the red-hot metal as she ran toward the mouth of the cave, exposing her sizzling flesh to the cool mountain air. Ignoring the pain that coursed through her arm, she grabbed one of the larger rocks from the cave-in and threw it directly at Regin's head.

The dragon was able to duck his head, but not so the rest of his body, and the rock struck his back. Crying out, Regin flopped to the plateau with an impact that knocked Sif off balance and sent her tumbling to the ground.

As Sif got to her feet, Regin's tail slithered across the rocky ground and collided with her ankles. Crashing back down, the upended Sif landed on her right side.

The entire mountain swam before her eyes. She tried to regain her feet, but the world swam even more every time she moved her head.

Closing her eyes helped, but then she couldn't see her foe.

But opening her eyes made it worse, so she closed them again.

She lay down her head on the cold ground. She needed just a moment, and then she would be fine.

If only her ears would stop ringing and the world would stop moving, she could defeat Regin.

"Sif!"

The voice was familiar and distant.

She risked opening her eyes.

Hilde stood over her.

"H-Hilde?"

"You gotta get up, the black dragon is going to kill that man!"

Gathering up every ounce of willpower, Sif propped herself up on her elbows.

She saw that Regin was looming over Oter, who was standing defiantly against the ridge.

Oter cried out in his lisping voice, "What are you waiting for? Kill me!"

"No need to rush, brother."

"Yes, there is. You must protect the hoard at all costs from any who would take it from you. Yet, you hesitate to kill me."

Regin simply continued looming. "I do not understand. I know I wish to finally kill you after all these years, but I cannot *feel* the emotions any longer."

"No, and you never will. Do you know why, Regin?" Oter

laughed. "Because I don't *want* the treasure! I'm no threat to your precious hoard! It's *all* yours! And *that* is all the curse cares about! Your own desires mean *nothing*, Regin. All that you are now is protector of your treasure. And since I am just a pathetic naked man cowering behind a ridge, the curse knows I pose no threat—and so you *won't* kill me. You *can't* kill me!" He shook his head. "Congratulations, Regin. You had the opportunity to live a new life, away from Father and his abuse, away from me and my curse. You had the skills and the freedom to continue the family business, or perhaps start a new one. Anything! Your options were as limitless as the Nine Worlds themselves! Instead, you wasted all this time trying to find me, just to ruin your own life the same way I ruined mine."

While Oter ranted at his confused brother, Sif closed her eyes and tried to focus her mind. Then, she slowly got to her feet. Hilde stood next to her, arms outstretched to help, though she hardly had the strength to hold Sif up.

After she got herself upright, Sif realized that Hilde wasn't trying to provide physical aid. Rather, she had something in her hands.

Squinting to clear her vision, Sif realized that it was her sword!

She snatched it from Hilde's grasp. "How did you find this?" That led her to a more pressing question. "Why are you here?"

"When I got back to Flodbjerge, I went to check on Regin like you asked—but he was gone. I tracked him to the mountains, and I thought he might be going after his brother. I found the sword on my way up."

"Thank you, Hilde," Sif said. "Now you must go and hide. The curse may realize that Oter is no threat, but it is unlikely to provide the same consideration for you and me."

Hilde nodded, and ran the opposite way on the plateau.

Sif raised her sword with her right arm, ignoring the agony of the burnt flesh. "Regin!"

Craning his neck around to look at Sif, Regin chuckled. "You're still alive, milady? Perhaps you are indeed made of sterner stuff than I thought." Then he once again breathed his flame.

Sif tried to dodge the fire, but her movements were tentative at best, and again she was burnt—this time on both her legs.

"Today is your day, Lady Sif!" Regin cried. "Today is the day that you fall to the sons of Hreidmar!"

Oter spit. "Do not include me in your idiocy, Regin!"

"But I must credit you, brother, for the Lady Sif moves slowly and poorly—all due to your own efforts against her."

Snarling, Sif ran toward the dragon, brandishing her sword. Regin, though, took to the air, and Sif was unable even to strike his tail as the creature flew upward.

Undaunted, Sif again grabbed a rock from the ground—

the plateau was now littered with them thanks to Regin's forceful exit from the cave—and threw it with all her waning strength at Regin's head.

This time, the dragon was unable to dodge, and the projectile struck the side of his snout. Dazed, Regin crashed to the plateau.

Again, the impact knocked Sif off balance, but she was able to use her sword to maintain her footing.

Splayed out on the plateau, tail draped over the ridge, Regin muttered, "Damn you . . ."

Sif responded through clenched teeth, as every step had become agony in her fatigue and pain. "No, Regin, you damned yourself."

She strode to the dragon's side and stood before his left wing. Raising her sword, she sliced downward, severing the wing completely.

Regin's screams echoed throughout the mountains and ichor spurted everywhere, while flame spewed from the creature's maw.

One burst of flame headed straight for Oter, who, eyes widening in panic, dove and rolled on the ground by the ridge.

Sif ran back toward the cave. She climbed up the collapsed rocks, gold, and jewels mixed with the broken stone, and onto the top of the cave.

Looking toward the ridge, she saw that Oter was not moving, and a trickle of blood flowed from underneath his head.

Glancing the other way, she saw Hilde hiding behind a rock. Sif was thankful that the girl was safe, at least. While she wished Hilde had remained in Flodbjerge, she had to admit to being grateful to have her sword back.

The dragon clambered to his feet and stumbled toward the cave.

"You . . . will . . . die . . . this . . . day . . ."

As Sif had hoped, Regin climbed up toward her. Though her legs were badly burnt by his fire, she managed to jump into the air just as the dragon tried to pounce upon her.

She came down and drove her sword into Regin's side. Where her blade had barely managed to penetrate Oter's hide, Regin's hide was as weak as his brother had told her it would be, and the sword went straight through.

Regin collapsed onto the pile of rock and gold.

"Hooray!" came Hilde's voice from below. "You won, Sif, you won!"

"Not quite." Sif's voice was ragged and breathy, and she was barely able to remain upright.

"What do you mean?" Hilde asked, confused.

Sif jumped down from her spot on top of both dragon and cave, the impact making her burnt limbs hurt even more.

"We must take him from his hoard, as I did Oter." She walked over to the dragon's tail, and again started to pull.

As weakened as she'd been after defeating Oter, she was now even weaker—but she had to complete her task. Oter and Regin both had to face Odin's justice, but they would face it as humans—not cursed dragons.

And so she gripped the dragon's tail and pulled.

"The measure of a warrior is not in songs that are sung."

Spots danced before her eyes, but she pulled.

"Warriors will ever be judged by how they fight, and how they win."

The pain in her right arm and in her feet turned the world into a haze, but she pulled.

"And I have always fought."

Next to her, Hilde grabbed a piece of the tail and pulled, as well.

"And I have always won."

Had Sif been buoyed by Hilde's assistance into greater feats of strength? Had Volstagg's daughter provided just enough extra muscle? Sif had no idea—but together, the two of them were able to drag Regin from his treasure.

Moments later, Regin's gaunt form lay once again before them.

With one rather large difference. No longer did Regin have a left arm.

Sif looked down at Hilde. The girl looked up at her from underneath her mop of red hair and smiled.

Satisfied that her work was done, Sif collapsed, blackness enveloping her at last.

CHAPTER TWELVE

When Sif finally awakened, she lay on a pallet indoors—which confused her, as her last memory was of standing on a plateau in the Valhalla Mountains.

Confusing her even more was the bearded face of Volstagg looking down on her and smiling.

"About time you woke up!"

"V-Volstagg? What are you doing here?" She looked around, seeing that she was in a small home. "What am I doing here? Where am I?"

"Which query would you like me to answer first?" Volstagg asked with a chuckle.

"None, actually, as I would much rather know how I came down from the mountain."

Sif pulled herself upright on the pallet, but her head swam as she did, so she quickly laid back down.

Volstagg's avuncular smile turned to a concerned frown as he put a comforting hand on her shoulder. "Rest, fair Sif, as your injuries are quite severe. The local healer says you are not yet ready to move."

Sif looked down and only then registered that her armor had been removed and replaced with a simple gown. Her right arm and both legs were covered in a white salve, which she assumed was to treat her burns.

The door to the house opened, and Hilde walked in, carrying a basket. "Father, I brought lunch for—" Then she noticed that the bed's occupant's eyes were open. "Sif! You're finally awake!"

"So it would seem. Your father was about to inform me as to how I got here."

"Indeed, I was," said Volstagg. "And my dear daughter has been kind enough to provide food, for what is a story without victuals to accompany it?"

Sif rolled her eyes. "Is there anything in your life that does not have victuals to accompany it?"

Grinning, Volstagg said, "Not if I may help it. Come, Hilde, lay out the fine repast you have provided, and I will tell Sif of what transpired while she slumbered."

"It was hardly a slumber," Sif muttered—but she was glad for the food, at least, as she was hungry enough to challenge Volstagg's gluttony.

Hilde sat on the floor, and Volstagg did likewise. (The house shook a bit when the Voluminous One's posterior collided with the floor, reminding Sif of when Oter had impacted with the earth on the mountain.) While Hilde spread out the food on a blanket, Volstagg commenced his tale.

"The story for me begins back in Asgard, when I went

to check on Hilde. You see, she and her brother had gotten into a bit of a spat, and had been confined to their rooms by their mother. Alaric, at least, obeyed her wishes." That last was said with a glower at the girl.

Hilde shrank a bit. "I'm sorry, Father, but Alaric took the hunting knife that—"

Volstagg held up a hand. "Yes, Hilde, I'm aware. Your mother told me. We will discuss *that* at another time."

"I take it," Sif said as she swallowed a fruit slice, "that you followed Hilde here?"

"Your brother was kind enough to inform me of Hilde's movements."

"Heimdall knew where I was?" Hilde asked, as if that was a surprise.

"Very little escapes the guardian's notice," Volstagg said with mock sternness. "You would do well to remember that in future."

Testily, Sif said, "Thus far, Volstagg, you have told me little of which I am not already aware."

"Patience, Sif, the Lion of Asgard will arrive at the heart of the tale in due course."

"No doubt, but I wish to still be young when that momentous event occurs."

Volstagg's belly quivered as he laughed heartily before downing a sweetmeat. "I traversed the Gopul River and reached Flodbjerge in due course. Upon my arrival, I was told that my daughter was last seen going to investigate the storehouse to check on a person named Regin, who was apparently the target of a dragon. But at the storehouse itself, I saw only a great deal of fish and felt a great deal of cold. And so I departed, confused, but then saw flame issuing forth from atop one of the Valhalla Mountains."

Hilde's eyes widened. "You *saw* that?"

"My vision may not be as keen as Heimdall's, but even these old orbs may espy flames gouting forth from a place where flames rarely are seen."

Sif regarded Volstagg with a skeptical expression. "Do not attempt to convince me that you hauled your bulk up that mountain."

Drawing himself up to his full height as best he could while sitting on a floor, Volstagg said, "I assure you, Sif, that were I to set my mind to the task, I would be able to scale the mountain with greater ease than you!" His face softened. "However, that proved unnecessary, thanks to my daughter. For even as I approached the foot of the mountain from the bottom, so too was she approaching it from above! And she was not alone."

Sif turned her gaze upon Hilde.

The girl turned away, blushing. "I found a hollowed-out tree near the stream, and I placed you, Oter, and Regin inside it. I used the rope that Regin used to tie up you and

Oter to secure the three of you in the tree, and then I pulled you down the mountain using the end of the rope. It took a while, but I managed it eventually."

At that, Sif gaped. "I am impressed, Hilde. That took ingenuity, courage, and strength."

"No, it didn't." Hilde smiled. "I just tried to figure out what *you* would do."

Snorting, Sif said, "In truth, I would have thrown both brothers down the mountain and left them to the Fates."

Volstagg continued the tale. "Hilde and the town council then filled me in on the entire story. I immediately sent a messenger to the dwarves to ascertain the original owner of the gold, since leaving it in anyone else's hands would merely perpetuate the curse."

Sif nodded. "Yes, thank you, Volstagg. Where are Oter and Regin now?"

"Imprisoned and under guard by the citizens of Flodbjerge. There is little love lost there, I can assure you. I have already volunteered Fandral and Hogun to assist in the village's rebuilding efforts."

"When I am well, I will do likewise."

Sternly, Volstagg said, "You will do no such thing. You are injured, and you will heal yourself. Besides, by the time you are well, we will be long done!"

Sif chuckled and shook her head.

Volstagg added, "And when you are well, we shall all return to the Realm Eternal with Oter and Regin as our prisoners. They will face the All-Father's justice."

Sif nodded. "I hope he will be lenient with Oter. He has suffered much, living with the curse so long, and I doubt any punishment Odin could visit upon him would be worse than the memory of what he endured as a dragon."

"If you argue so, fair Sif," Volstagg said, "then it will be like to come true."

Helena opened the door and asked, "How is our hero? Ah, awake, I see! It is good to see you improving, milady."

"Thank you, Helena, it is good to be so seen."

A dwarf walked in behind her. Helena said, "This is Engin. He is the son of Andvari, the dwarf from whom Oter and Regin stole the gold."

"My father," the dwarf said, "is old and infirm, and unable to make the journey, but I gladly come in his place, knowing that my return will mean his redemption."

"Welcome, Engin," Sif said.

"You must be the Lady Sif. Helena has spoken very highly of you. She says that you saved this village from the dragons my father had cursed. Thank you." He looked at Helena. "In exchange, madam, I wish to bequeath half the gold to your village—after removing the curse, of course. Use it to rebuild your town and restore it to its former glory."

Helena was visibly taken aback. "That is—that is very generous, sir."

"Consider it a finder's fee. In truth, Andvari had long since given up on ever seeing his gold again. All his dreams for how he would live out the remainder of his life were tied up in that coin, and the loss of it devastated him. Even receiving half of it back will buoy him more than words can say—but he will not object to you good people receiving a share, as the curse he left on it is what led to the tragedies that have befallen you. A contingent of my people are en route, and they will remove both the gold and the curse within the week."

Sif nodded. "Please, Engin, when you excavate the treasure from the collapsed cave, be you on the lookout for a sword. It belongs to one of the council, a fine man named Bjorn. He loaned me the blade—named Gunnvarr—and I would see it returned to him intact."

"I will see it done, milady."

"You are a good man, Engin."

"I but follow the example of the Lady Sif," Engin said with a bow. "I, at least, have something to gain by my generosity—I will receive half a fortune, and see my father returned to the man he was before the theft of his wealth. You had nothing to gain, yet you gave of yourself—risking your life—so that these people might be safe. I heard Helena refer to you as her hero—and to my mind, this makes you the finest hero of the Nine Worlds."

Sif smiled. "I daresay that many others may also qualify for such a title, but I would never object to being in their company." With looks at both Volstagg and Hilde, she added, "I am in the company of some right now, in fact." She looked at Helena and Engin. "But I am being a poor host. Hilde has gathered a feast for us. Please do join us, lest Volstagg eat it all."

"Of course!" Volstagg said with a hearty laugh. "Food is best shared amongst friends, after all!"

Hilde stared at him. "Since when have you ever *shared* food, Father?"

They all laughed at that. Helena and Engin took their places on the floor and everyone joined in the feast.

THE END

MARVEL

WARRIORS THREE

GODHOOD'S END

*Read on for a sneak peek at the
next installment of Marvel's Tales of
Asgard Trilogy from Joe Books.*

At the center of the Nine Worlds is Yggdrasil, the world tree, linking all of the worlds all via its mighty roots and powerful branches.

Thousands of years ago, the Aesir of Asgard did cross the rainbow bridge, the Bifrost, to Midgard, which its inhabitants call Earth. The people of Midgard did view the powerful warriors of Asgard as gods, and many did worship them as such.

The thunder god, Thor—son and heir to Odin, ruler of the gods of Asgard—had once been a callow youth, though he has since grown to become a fine warrior. Upon proving himself worthy, he was awarded Mjolnir, the mighty Uru hammer that thenceforth became his trademark weapon.

This night marked the eve of a journey to Ydalir, a section of Asgard on which trolls were encroaching. Honoring the Aesir's tradition, Thor held a feast for his comrades in arms in Bilskirnir, the great hall Odin had gifted to him not long after granting him Mjolnir.

One of those comrades was Fandral, with whom Thor had trained in the art of swordplay with the thunder god's older half brother, Tyr.

Another was Volstagg, who was much older than Thor, and had been a decorated war chieftain in Thrudheim.

Fandral was regaling some of the others with tales of his death-defying battle against Thrivaldi, the thrice-mighty. "With my longsword, I did pop out one of the beast's eyes—and then with a second thrust, out came the other. The beast's head could see no more!"

Fandral paused for effect. "A pity, then, that the beast had nine heads. For Thrivaldi was called 'the thrice-mighty' with good cause! Had he only the three heads, he would simply be 'the mighty.'"

When Fandral was done with his tale, Volstagg stepped forward. Thor had been a boy when he first met Volstagg, who had then carried a trim, muscular figure. Now, though, his form had become a bit rounded, and Thor did note that his plate was far fuller than that of anyone else in the hall. Nonetheless, he still stood taller than any in the room. "If there's anything I cannot bear," he said of Fandral, "it is a warrior who exaggerates his accomplishments!"

A young man named Hogun, who had only recently come to Asgard, spoke softly. "I have heard many of your tales, Volstagg. They are far less believable than Fandral's."

"Nonsense! Truly did I slay the Utgard Boar with my bare hands!"

Hogun frowned. "I seem to recall that when you told me the story on the night we met, you had used your sword."

Fandral laughed. "In truth, kind Hogun, I suspect the braggart did slay the boar solely that he might add him to his feast."

Volstagg glanced down at his plate, laden with a varied sampling of the victuals available in Thor's hall. "Do not mistake appetite for indolence, young braggart."

"Nor do I mistake you for a warrior! Were it not for your friendship with Thor, I doubt you would even be permitted to sit at the high table in Odin's banquet hall."

Thor had up to that point stayed out of the conversation. While he did not know Hogun well, he numbered both Volstagg and Fandral amongst his friends. But at this slight, he did join in. "Hold, Fandral, your words cut me to the quick, and do likewise to the All-Father. None may sit at Odin's table who are not worthy."

To his credit, Fandral looked abashed, and he bowed low. "My apologies, Thor, I meant no offense. I mean only to say that when I sit at the high table, I shall truly earn it!"

"Pfah." Volstagg idly grabbed a piece of meat off his plate and stuffed it into his bearded face. "I find that very unlikely. Were you able to beard Svafnir in its lair?"

"With my eyes closed," Fandral said with a chortle. "Were you able to defeat the monstrous sea serpents in the river that flows on either side of the Isle of Love?"

"No," Volstagg replied, "but only because I have no need to travel to such an island, as love is my constant companion."

"Given your love of food, that surprises me not," Fandral said nastily.

Volstagg slammed a fist on the table. "I speak of my noble wife, Gudrun! The finest flower in all of Asgard!"

Thor quickly stepped in before his two friends came to blows. "Hogun, why do you not regale us with a tale of your own?"

The dark-haired youth quickly shook his head. "Nay, my prince, I have no such tale to tell."

"Not even the story of how you came to fair Asgard?"

Hogun allowed himself a small smile. "I walked, sire. And eventually did arrive here, where now I am apprentice to a stonemason, with hopes of becoming an artisan."

Volstagg ate another morsel, this off Thor's plate, and Fandral sneered. "Does this Gudrun not feed you that you must eat everything in sight?"

Whirling on Fandral, Volstagg cried, "Do not again speak ill of my beloved wife! I was slaying trolls when you were still in swaddling clothes!"

"Boring them to death with your boasts, no doubt."

"Do not mistake my exploits for boasts, boy. Such is my might and cunning that I could travel to Niffleheim, pat Fenris on the head, and not lose a fingernail in the doing of it!"

Fandral snorted derisively. "Not before I did it first, ponderous one!"

Seeing an opportunity to end the argument, Thor said, "A wager! What better end to my feast than a quest that will resolve a bet between warriors?"

"Then it shall be done!" Fandral cried. "I will show this fool for the popinjay that he is!"

Volstagg nodded. "We will leave at first light."

Thor winced. "Alas, I may not accompany you, as we ride to Ydalir tomorrow."

"But you must come!" Fandral said. "We needs must have someone impartial to judge the competition."

Looking at the young, dark-haired man, Thor asked, "What of Hogun?"

"Yes!" Volstagg said. "I would trust Hogun to be fair about it when I am victorious."

Fandral glared at Volstagg, then smiled at Hogun. "He is friend to us both and therefore loyal to neither exclusively. While there is little on which I would agree with Volstagg, I do agree that Hogun is a good lad."

Hogun bowed his head. "I would be honored."

"Then it's settled," Thor said.

Fandral grinned. "Be you at the docks of Ormt at first light, Voluminous One—if you've still a belly for this once you've sobered up."

Volstagg laughed derisively. "I'll be there, child. Just don't make me drag you out from behind your mother's skirts come daybreak."

And so it came to pass the following morning that they met at the docks of Ormt.

Fandral thought of the glory that would be his when he made a fool of old Volstagg.

Volstagg thought of the meal that Gudrun had packed for him, all the while muttering about her idiot husband going on fool quests when there were chores to be performed.

Hogun kept his thoughts to himself.

They set sail for Niffleheim as the sun rose, and ere long they came to the shores of that land of the dishonored dead.

Though only the bravest or the most foolhardy traverse from one world to the other, it was an open question which description applied to the old warrior, the young swordsman, and the quiet boy.

Along the way, Volstagg told Hogun the story of Fenris.

"Fenris is a giant wolf—the child of Thor's adoptive brother, Loki, and the giant Angerboda. Loki, I must say, has the most bizarre offspring. In any event, Fenris was too dangerous to be allowed to roam unfettered, and so Odin decreed that he be bound."

Fandral interrupted the story. "It was more complicated than that, of course, because no bond could hold the giant wolf. And, the wolf is wily and not easily trapped. It was my former teacher, Tyr, who finally was able to bind him—though at the cost of his hand."

Now Volstagg interrupted. "It was more complicated than *that*, of course."

Fandral sneered.

Volstagg went on. "The wolf could not be held by any bond created by Asgard, and so the All-Father did as he often would when he needed craftwork—he traveled to Nidavellir and commissioned the dwarves. They, who forged so many weapons—from Thor's hammer to Balder's shield—easily could construct a leash for Fenris."

"And they created Gleipnir," Fandral continued. "So thin as to be invisible, so sharp as to slice in two any object, it remains wrapped around the neck of Fenris. Should he strain Gleipnir too far, his head will be cut from his body."

Hogun frowned. "Then why is he so dangerous?"

"To be close enough to pat him on the head is to be close enough to be mauled by him," Fandral said.

Volstagg added, "Plus, as I said, he is wily."

"Actually, *I* said that," Fandral replied angrily.

Ignoring him, Volstagg said, "He will try to trick us into removing Gleipnir."

When they arrived at the misty plains of Niffleheim, they were beset upon almost immediately by a half-dozen Ice Giants, who served Ymir.

Before Fandral could react, Volstagg moved upon them, wielding his blade with tremendous strength; for while Volstagg's size was only partly muscle—his middle starting to grow larger as he aged—he remained the Lion of Asgard.

He broke three of the Ice Giants in two with his might, and beheaded the other three.

"I must confess, Volstagg," Fandral said slowly, "I did not believe you had such fire in you for aught save feasting."

Volstagg's response came between ragged breaths, for in truth the effort had fatigued him more than expected. "The Lion of Asgard is a man of passion, child, in all things. Now let us continue—Fenris awaits!"

They moved onward, but were again stopped on the misty roads of Niffleheim—this time by a rock troll.

"Smell Aesir, I believed I did," the rock troll rumbled. "Die, you will, by the hand of Glarin of the Sword!"

Hogun's eyes went wide. "I have heard tales of Glarin of the Sword. It is said that none may defeat him as long as he grips his blade."

Fandral simply grinned, holding his own sword aloft. "You obviously misheard, good Hogun, for that is what is said of me!"

"First, you shall be, blond one," the rock troll said. "Your comrades, next."

"Hardly." Fandral ran toward Glarin. "Have at thee!"

The sword fight was the greatest in which Fandral had ever engaged. Never before had he been so challenged, not even in his earliest days training under Tyr.

Every thrust of Fandral's, Glarin did counter. Every strike of Glarin's, Fandral was barely able to parry.

Only after a seeming eternity of fighting did Fandral note that Glarin occasionally left open his right side. It was but for a moment when he did an upward thrust, and it took Fandral several tries before he even could attempt to take advantage of it.

But eventually, he did so, slicing his blade through the rock troll's leg.

Glarin of the Sword cried in agony as a filthy ichor spewed from his earthen skin.

"Wound me, you have! Never before this has happened!"

"And never again shall it happen," Fandral said as he cleaved Glarin's head from the rest of his rocky body.

"Impressive, young Fandral," Volstagg said. "Never before have I seen such swordplay—not even my own."

Fandral bowed, before continuing to clean his sword. "The Lion of Asgard does me privilege."

"You are both great warriors," Hogun said. "It is my honor to judge your competition."

"Yes." Volstagg said the word quietly, and he briefly became lost in thought before brightening once more. "Come! The wolf awaits!"

Farther they did travel, and soon reached the third root of Yggdrasil that linked Niffleheim to the rest of the Nine Worlds. Gnawing at the root was a giant green dragon.

"'Tis Nidhogg," Fandral whispered almost reverently.

"I have heard tell," Hogun also whispered, "that he gnaws on both the root of the world tree and the souls of the dishonored dead."

Volstagg, uncharacteristically, said nothing. He had hoped they would be able to avoid the wyrm, that it would be too occupied with its gluttonous task to be concerned with two warriors and a lad.

But it was not to be. As soon as they approached, the dragon reared back its scaly head.

"Run! Quickly!"

At Volstagg's urging, the three moved as fast as their legs would carry them.

Nidhogg, though, needed no legs to move, for he had wings, and he did use them to overtake Fandral and Volstagg in an instant.

Helplessly, Hogun watched as his friends were slammed to the ground and held there by Nidhogg's mighty claws.

"R-run, Hogun! Save—save yourself!" Volstagg uttered as the dragon's claw crushed his massive frame.

Fandral, equally strained, added, "No sense in all three of us dying! Return to Asgard! Tell them we fought valiantly!"

For several seconds, Hogun simply stared as he watched both of his friends, brought low by the dragon.

And for a moment, he saw in his mind's eye two other people dear to him who had been crushed by the might of a massive creature. He had been frightened then, unable to act. He had sworn never again to put himself in such a position.

Yet here he was, and he would *not* let Volstagg and Fandral suffer the same fate as his cousins.

Unsheathing the dagger that was all he had left from his father, Hogun cried out in anguish and attacked.

Nidhogg had not even acknowledged Hogun, perceiving him as unarmed and not a threat. That proved a dangerous mistake, as Hogun plunged his father's dagger into the creature's wing.

Screaming with an unearthly howl, Nidhogg did then fly away brokenly, unwilling to work so hard for food when Niffleheim provided all he desired without effort. More souls would try to escape Hel soon enough, and Nidhogg needed only to be ready to consume them. These two—or, rather, three—warriors had seemed a decent distraction, but not enough to keep the dragon from his task.

Hogun helped Fandral to his feet. Volstagg clambered upward of his own accord.

"You have the thanks of the Lion of Asgard," Volstagg said.

"And the confusion of both of us, I would think," Fandral added. "I thought you an aspiring artisan?"

"I was," Hogun said quietly. "I prevaricated last night when I told Thor that I had no story to tell of coming to

Asgard beyond that I walked. In truth, my tribe was massacred and our standard stolen by a creature known as Mogul of the Mystic Mountain."

Volstagg nodded. "I've heard tales of that tyrant, but always believed them to be false—and Mogul himself but a legend."

"He is no legend, Volstagg," Hogun said bitterly. "He killed my family and scattered my tribe. I know not how many still live, if any. My twin cousins and I survived. They were older than I, and noble warriors. They attempted to do battle against Mogul, but his slave, the Jinni giant, did take their lives. I froze, unable to help them."

Volstagg put a hand on Hogun's shoulder, but the young man shrugged it off.

"You were but a youth," Volstagg said, "who saw his family destroyed. There is no shame in fear, young Hogun, especially in one untrained—"

"I *was* trained! You do not understand, Volstagg—I was raised to be a warrior and weapon smith, like my father." Hogun held up the dagger, still dripping with Nidhogg's blood. "He crafted this dagger as a gift for me after I made my first kill. But when I saw my dear cousins laid low by the Jinni, I forgot all my training and saw only death. And so I ran." He looked up at Fandral and Volstagg. "I swore never to put myself in such a position again. I came to Asgard, where I knew I could lose myself amongst the Aesir and use my smithing skills to become an artisan."

"Then why did you come with us?" Fandral asked.

"For the same reason I befriended you both, and wished to do so with Thor."

Volstagg spoke with grave understanding. "You may take the boy out of the warrior, but you may not take the warrior out of the boy. You heard the siren call of battle."

Hogun nodded. "Still, I thought I could keep to my vow. I was merely to judge which of you would pet the Fenris Wolf's pelt first. But when I saw you both in danger, just as my cousins were—"

"Then you acted," Fandral said with a grin. "The measure of a warrior lies not merely in his victories, but also in how he recovers from defeat. After all, even the finest warrior may lose a battle—it is only the poor ones who lose the same way twice."

Volstagg regarded Fandral with amusement. "That almost approached profundity, boy." But he spoke with none of the previous night's acrimony.

"Your words are kind," Hogun said grimly, "but still, I have broken my vow. And had I not, I would have let two good men die. I see no good in any of this."

"I see one good," Volstagg said. "I see us. Last night we were three fools in a feasting hall. Today, we are three warriors out to make a fool of the Fenris Wolf. But hang our wager—instead, we shall work together, the three of us, to pat Fenris on the head and live to tell the tale!"

"Agreed," Fandral said with a smile.

Hogun did not smile, but he did nod. "Agreed, as well. Let us beard the wolf together."

And so the Warriors Three did march into danger for the first, but far from the last, time . . .

ACKNOWLEDGMENTS

The number of people who deserve thanks for this book are legion, and I hope I manage to get all of them in. I will start with the folks at Joe Books: Robert Simpson (who first approached me with this), Adam Fortier, Stephanie Alouche, Amy Weingartner, and especially my noble editors, Rob Tokar and Paul Taunton.

Huge thanks, as always, to my amazing agent Lucienne Diver, who kept the paperwork mills grinding and more than earned her commission.

Of course, this trilogy owes a ton to the comic books featuring the various Asgardians that Marvel has published since 1962, and while I don't have the space to thank *all* the creators of those comics, I want to single out a few. First off, Stan Lee, Larry Lieber, Jack Kirby, and Joe Sinnott, who created this incarnation of Thor and his chums in *Journey Into Mystery* #83. Secondly, and most especially, the great Walt Simonson, whose run on *Thor* from 1983 to 1987 (as well as the *Balder the Brave* miniseries), aided and abetted by Sal Buscema and John Workman Jr., is pretty much the text, chapter, and verse of "definitive." Thirdly, Kelly Sue DeConnick, Ryan Stegman, Kathryn Immonen, and Valerio Schiti, who chronicled solo adventures for Sif in the *Sif* one-shot and *Journey Into Mystery* #646-655. In addition, I must give thanks and praise to the following excellent creators whose work was particularly influential on this trilogy: Jason Aaron, Pierce Askegren, Joe Barney, John Buscema, Kurt Busiek, Gerry Conway, Russell Dauterman, Tom DeFalco, Ron Frenz, Michael Jan Friedman, Gary Friedrich, Mark Gruenwald, Stuart Immonen, Dan Jurgens, Gil Kane, Pepe Larraz, John Lewandowski, Ralph Macchio, Doug Moench, George Pérez, Don Perlin, Keith Pollard, John Romita Jr., Marie Severin, Roger Stern, Roy Thomas, Charles Vess, Len Wein, Bill Willingham, and Alan Zelenetz.

Also, while these novels are not part of the Marvel Cinematic Universe, I cannot deny the influence of the portrayals of the characters in the movies *Thor* and *Thor: The Dark World,* and on the TV show *Marvel's Agents of S.H.I.E.L.D.* (nor would I wish to deny it, as they were all superb), and so I must thank actors Chris Hemsworth, Sir Anthony Hopkins, Idris Elba, Ray Stevenson, and most especially Jaimie Alexander (who is the perfect Sif), as well as screenwriters Shalisha Francis, Drew Z. Greenberg, Christopher Markus, Stephen McFeely, Ashley Edward Miller, Don Payne, Mark Protosevich, Robert Rodat, Zack Stentz, J. Michael Straczynski, and Christopher Yost.

Also, one can't write anything about the Norse gods without acknowledging the work of the great Snorri Sturluson, without whom we wouldn't know jack about the Aesir. In particular, I made use of the *Völsunga Saga*, which recounts the original story of the dragons on which this novel is based. Additional thanks must go to Saxo Grammaticus, from whose *Gesta Danorum* I (very, very liberally) adapted Sif's tale of her battle against the Lindworm of Denmark.

Thanks to my noble first reader, the mighty GraceAnne Andreassi DeCandido (a.k.a. The Mom). And thanks to Wrenn Simms, Dale Mazur, Meredith Peruzzi, Tina Randleman, and especially Robert Greenberger for general wonderfulness, as well as the various furred folks in my life, Kaylee, Louie, and the dearly departed Scooter and Elsa.

ABOUT THE AUTHOR

K eith R.A. DeCandido has a long history with Marvel characters in prose. From 1994 to 2000, Boulevard Books published more than fifty Marvel novels and short-story anthologies, for which Keith served as the editorial director. Keith also contributed on the writing side, penning short stories for the anthologies *The Ultimate Spider-Man, The Ultimate Silver Surfer, Untold Tales of Spider-Man, The Ultimate Hulk,* and *X-Men Legends,* and collaborating with José R. Nieto on the novel *Spider-Man: Venom's Wrath.* In 2005, Keith wrote a stand-alone book for Simon & Schuster titled *Spider-Man: Down These Mean Streets.*

The Tales of Asgard trilogy isn't Keith's first foray into Norse myth, either, having written a cycle of urban fantasy stories set in Key West, Florida, that feature a young woman named Cassie Zukav, a Dís—one of the fate goddesses— who encounters many characters from the Norse pantheon (including Thor, Loki, Tyr, and Odin). Those stories can be found in the online zines *Buzzy Mag* and *Story of the Month Club,* in the anthologies *Apocalypse 13, Bad-Ass Faeries: It's Elemental, Out of Tune, Tales from the House Band* Volumes 1 & 2, *TV Gods: Summer Programming,* and *Urban Nightmares,* and in the short-story collections *Ragnarok and Roll: Tales of Cassie Zukav, Weirdness Magnet* and *Without a License: The Fantastic Worlds of Keith R.A. DeCandido.*

Keith's other work includes tie-in fiction based on TV shows (*Star Trek, Supernatural, Doctor Who, Sleepy Hollow*), games (*World of Warcraft, Dungeons & Dragons, StarCraft, Command and Conquer*), and films (*Serenity, Resident Evil, Disney Cars*), as well as original fiction, most notably the "Precinct" series of high fantasy police procedurals that includes five novels (*Dragon Precinct, Unicorn Precinct, Goblin Precinct, Gryphon Precinct*, and the forthcoming *Mermaid Precinct*) and more than a dozen short stories. Some of his other recent and upcoming work includes the *Stargate SG-1* novel *Kali's Wrath*, the *Star Trek* coffee-table book *The Klingon Art of War*, the *Sleepy Hollow* novel *Children of the Revolution*, the *Heroes Reborn* novella *Save the Cheerleader, Destroy the World*, the *Super City Police Department* serial novella *Avenging Amethyst*, and short stories in the anthologies *X-Files: Trust No One, V-Wars: Night Terrors, With Great Power, Limbus, Inc.* Book 3, *The Side of Good/The Side of Evil*, and *Nights of the Living Dead* (edited by George Romero and Jonathan Maberry).

Keith is also a freelance editor, a veteran anthologist, a professional musician (currently with the parody band Boogie Knights, one of whose songs is called "Ragnarok"), a second-degree black belt in karate (in which he both trains and teaches), a rabid fan of the New York Yankees, and probably some other stuff that he can't remember because of lack of sleep. He lives in New York City with folks both bipedal and quadrupedal. Find out less at his hopelessly out-of-date website, DeCandido.net, which is the gateway to his online footprint.